**The Atharannach of Alba
by Matt Parrott**

© 2012 by Matthew Parrott

All rights reserved. This book or any portion thereof may not be reproduced or used in any manner whatsoever without the express written permission of the publisher except for the use of brief quotations where required, i.e. book reviews.

To all the members of the *Haggis!* tour which so inspired this book, and were amongst the first people to ever encourage me to take writing seriously.

Also to Will and Amy: without whom I would never have had the courage to continue writing.

The Seventh Bed

A cold wind drifted in through the flimsy doors that marked the entrance to the Aloysius building. Halfway down the corridor a woman mopping the tiled floor gave a shudder and her grip on the mop loosened causing it to plummet back down into the bucket. The foamy water within surged like a wave breaking against rocks and crashed onto the iceberg blue walls, darkening them and making them drip as if the hand-painted clouds above had released their stock of children's tears and were now raining onto the woman below.

'BUGGER!' said the woman, dressed in a khaki uniform that was now mottled with soap and patches of damp.

'Thank God there's only ten minutes left of this shift!' she shouted, 'Stinkin'' place can't even afford proper doors! And these,' she banged her mop forcefully on the floor, '..these tiles don't want mopping, they want rippin' up and startin' all again!!' and she shook her hand, replacing wet with cold.

'Everything alright Glenda?' called a deep voice.

'Aye..... just a slip is all,' the woman called back in an airy tone, before muttering under her breath: 'I mean if you paid me a bit more I'd understand....' She shook her head, slumping back over her mop.

Down the corridor and around the bend, two figures stood outside a room labelled 'A1'. One was a short, intellectual-looking man with thinning hair and glasses. The other was a beautiful young woman with bright red hair which fell in shining locks about her person and seemed to blend seamlessly into her fox-fur coat.

'Sorry about that; she's our cleaner,' said the man in a deep voice that didn't match his appearance. 'We've been having a bit of trouble with her lately. Think she's losing the plot.'

'Not at all,' replied the woman, tilting her head slightly. 'Shall we go in now?'

'Oh of course,' said the man, and fumbled with the keypad on the outside of the door, his fingers working faster than his brain. 'Sorry, just.... Ah here we go.' With a click, he swung the door open. 'After you.'

As the woman stepped over the threshold, the lights embedded in the corners of the ceiling automatically switched on, illuminating the room just enough to be able to determine the contents. Lined up against the back wall were seven wrought-iron cribs. Though each had originally been painted white, time and neglect had weathered them into a mottled shade, reminiscent of a pigeon in snow. From every crib, the silent breaths of innocence came deep and slow. A group-produced and group-appreciated lullaby which reduced even the rowdiest of adult visitors to statue-silence. Tied to the foot-end of each crib was a piece of laminated paper that displayed the child's date of birth, sex and, name.

Approaching the line-up, the pair of adults, invaders of dreams, softened their steps and walked gently beside the row, from right to left. The eyes of the man never left his companion for more than a moment; he was eager to find a home for one of his charges. One less mouth to feed. The woman, however, moved robotically. Her face devoid of emotion, she surveyed with precision the features of each sleeping babe, taking their blue or pink blankets as an indication of sex and looking carefully at each ticket, stopping at none for more than a few seconds.

When she reached the final crib, at the far left of the room, furthest from the door - her eyes widened slightly and, taking the ticket in her hand, she let the slightest grin cross her face.

Name: *Leo   [last unknown]*
Sex: *Male*
D.O.B: *1ˢᵗ August 1989*

'Beautiful isn't he?' whispered the man. 'Haven't seen that much hair on a child for a long time.'

This particular child, fast asleep in the seventh bed, was

quite unlike the rest of the children. Where the others had the usual ruddy complexion of babes, all rosy cheeks or soft dark skin and either had little or no hair - this child, this boy, was pale white with a head full of platinum blonde hair.

'And you should see his eyes.'

The woman's nostrils flared.

'So different from any I've ever seen before. His irises are white - outlined with a perfect ring of black. Our doctors think it's genetic, you know, like albinism. Yet he's quite healthy. Doesn't cry so much as the others perhaps, but then, who wants to be up at all hours anyway?' he chuckled. With this the woman swung her head round sharply.

'Yes,' she agreed, 'quite.' She let the grin fade from her lips, and allowed her body to turn.

'Listen, could you do me a favour?' she said, holding his eyes.

'Of course, anything, what is it?'

'I need to talk things over with my husband, and it might take a while. I'd love to have the boy but at the same time I wouldn't want him to miss out on getting a home sooner - I don't suppose you'd you be able to send me a letter if he does go? I should like to know that he gets on alright.'

'Absolutely... what's your address?' he asked, hoping in vain that she would include an invite alongside it.

'Helmsford Hall, Hertfordshire - that should be enough to get it there, with a stamp.'

'Yes, okay, done. I do hope you can come to an arrangement with your husband in time though.'

'Me too,' she smiled, her pure white teeth shining in the semi-darkness.

'Would you like to stay for a coffee? It's horrible out there at the moment, wouldn't want you to get stuck in your car overnight.'

Looking down at herself, the woman brushed her coat and checked her watch.

'Oh, no thank you, I really must be off.' She started towards the door and the man began to follow. 'No really, it's fine, I'll see myself out. Do keep me informed,' she said, and with one last look at the seventh bed, walked out of the door.

When she was alone, in the now Glenda-free corridor, she pulled herself up, shook her head slightly and let an enormous smile spread across her face. The cold of the building dissipated and she felt quite warm. Everyone would be so pleased with her.

'You should see his eyes,' she hissed.

'Leo!' she chuckled, 'Leo!'

Standing alone in room A1, the man surveyed the row of cribs and, shivering, pulled his cardigan tighter over him. He looked down at his notepad, the ink of the woman's address still not yet dry and the sinking feeling became a cannon-ball lodged in his throat. Coughing loudly in an attempt to stave off his tears of defeat, he shoved his notepad into his pocket and took one step forward to leave. It was then he noticed, glimmering on the hard stone floor, a tiny golden object. He bent down to retrieve it and played with it in his hands, scrunching up his eyes to see what it was. A long thin hook attached to the back of a lion. An earring.

'She must have dropped it!' he shouted, and clutching it in his palm, ran out through the door into the corridor. Bounding its length in a few seconds he pushed open the badly hung wooden doors and stepped out, panting, into the bitter night air. It was no use, she had gone. On either side of the access road was darkness, and all around the land was still and bleak, blanketed in sugarsnow. He played with the lion between his fingers and gazed up into the stars.

He would send it to her tomorrow. Passing the tiny, perfect lion from one hand to the next, he toyed with it in admiration. It was bound to have been expensive. She would miss it. He would send it by first post or-

'Maybe not,' he whispered. For in the collection of beautiful things, of jewellery, children and buildings; he had always sought to find a beauty of his own.

Turning into the doorway, he pocketed the earring and sighed.

The Lie

The view from the window of Hall & Sons newsagents and greengrocers changed little, day to day, season to season. In the daylight buses trundled by and residents passed in ones and twos; cars an infrequent but welcome distraction. The doors of the small shops and pubs lining the street would open and close and once-daily laughter, chatter and a flurry of black, navy and green uniforms would mark the arrival of the school buses. By night the street became an otherworld: dated streetlamps pumped out the glow of a coal fire's ember, shrouding the stone and tarmac in a basecoat of umber; over which the neon store lights painted their radioactive hues. Cars rushed past, eager to add their alkaline whites, reds and yellows to the canvas. An ecstasy of energy and a comforting warmth to witness behind a pane of glass: that other people were living their lives - that the world would continue to go on without you.

'Come on then! Can't be sitting around all night! We've still got to cash up.'

'Sorry Mum,' said Leo who'd been perched on the window ledge as he had so many times before.

Sandra Hall was a hard woman. Determined and ruthless, she never failed at anything. The success of her business built from nothing to exceptional profit in less than five years paid testament to this. She loathed the lazy and had little time for introverts.

'Right, no Leo, I want those left there. Just get out the broom and have a sweep will you? Oh and there's two boxes of Everyman's Potato Crisps out the back which will go out,' said Sandra, her tone dismissive and authoritarian.

'Yes Mum,' replied Leo and he walked to the corner of the store, beside the magazines and took a broom and dustpan and brush from the cupboard. As often happens when you've done a job countless times over countless years, Leo had fallen into a rhythm - a way of manoeuvring the entire store so as to remove as much dust and dirt as possible. He started first beside the magazines, then swept under the all the shelving towards the back wall and the vegetables, then repeated the process in reverse but this time sweeping the walkways. Regardless of how tired Leo was, of how many times he had run out to the stores and back again, or how long he'd been standing on his feet serving customer after customer he would always relish the last task of the day. 'Humility is good for the soul,' he would tell himself. His thoughts would wander to often unexpected places and he'd think he could hear singing.

This time however, the only singing to be heard was the ringing of the till. Sandra had been late cashing up and the printing churns and beeps of their brand new cash-register resounded from the wooden beams of the ceiling forcing Leo to accept the present.

'Oh-hoh-ho! We've done well today boy!!' said Sandra, her voice sing-songy and her face bright.

'How well Mum?' said Leo, never looking up from his broom.

'Let's just say I think we'll be able to afford that new car after all eh?'

'That's brilliant!'

'Yeah, it is, isn't it?, I must tell your Dad,' and she closed the cash register draw, ripped off the Z reading and shouted: 'Bob?! BOB!!!? Get down here and see how much we've done today!'

'Alrigh' Alrigh' hold your horses woman!' said a bodiless voice from just above the stairs which ran behind the counter. A few bangs later, much like the dull thud of a benchweight onto carpet and the slippered feet of Bob Hall appeared. The rest of his large body came slowly into view, the buttons of his blue shirt accentuating his large size, and a billow of smoke encircled his head like a carcinogenic halo. Both Bob and Sandra Hall smoked, but never tailor-made. When not otherwise involved they could often be seen employing the finest tobacco-origami techniques known to man.

Descending the final few steps, Bob retrieved the filthy roll-up from his mouth with his enormous hand and said: 'I was just getting into that, that fella from that Runaway film's on telly - some quiz showorother. What did you have t-'

'Ohhhh.. never mind about that,' said Sandra, and raised her hand to Bob's eyes -flaunting the piece of paper in front of them. Her tall, thin frame looked absurd with one hand on the counter and the other held up in front of her. She looked like she might be about to do a dance step. After grabbing her hand and pushing it away slightly, Bob's failing eyes found the figure he needed and his face looked as though it were about to explode. He clapped his hands together with a loud slap.

'Yessss!!!!' he hissed. 'No more second-rate *Audi*!' And he embraced his wife, who looked as if she might snap, and they both beamed with happiness.

Leo, who'd now finished the sweeping, was leaning on the broom and had joined in with the smiling. Though ultimately he wasn't too sure if he agreed with his parents consistent desire for more, nothing pleased him as much as seeing them happy - together. Any show of unity helped exorcise the demons of their past arguments which lodged into him like shrapnel, violent parasites sapping his sense of self away with every cross word.

'Will you turn the lights out?' Sandra said to Leo. 'We're gonna get an early night. Lots to do tomorrow.'

'Yeah, like getting to the showroom pronto,' added Bob, with a guffaw.

'Shhh, get up them stairs you!'

Grinning and shaking his head, Leo retrieved the dustpan and brush from the corner of the room where he'd left it and picked up the now sizeable pile of dust and detritus.

'Another day over,' he said quietly to himself as he scraped the pan into the bin and put all his things back into the cupboard. He turned on his heel and surveyed the shop, the counter, the brown paper bags, the hand-made 'Now Only' signs and the dent in the rusty brown tiles of the floor where he'd tripped up at the age of 6, scarred his leg and been told to 'Get up, wash the blood off the floor and be more careful in future'. He'd be 18 tomorrow. An adult, finally, and yet he had no idea where he was going. His parents wanted him to stay with the shop, to keep it going with, and after, them but the passion this inspired in him was similar to that felt by a baker watching a lawn rise. He yawned, rubbed his eyes with the palms of his hand and stretched out to the largest he could.

'Time for bed,' he sighed.

He climbed the stairs to the family living quarters, where the walls were lined with pink textured paper as soon as the stairway was out of sight of the shop and continued, like an enormous marshmallow, throughout the landing. On every wall were photographs of family holidays. One in Bali; one in New York; one in Egypt. Leo couldn't help but think to himself that these were more boastful symbol than tender memento. Stopping just before his bedroom, he flicked the switch that controlled the downstairs electrics and replaced the clear-plastic cover. Quickly he checked that neither the Living room nor the galley kitchen/bathroom lights were on before gently turning the handle on his matte white door.

'Alright?' said Jacob, lounging on a large leather chair at his computer desk. The only light in the room was coming from his screen, and it gave him the aura of a corpse. His eyes had flicked only momentarily towards Leo, and after he'd been acknowledged - returned to his computer game. Though Leo and Jacob were brothers, they could not have been less alike. Leo was pale and extremely fair haired whilst Jacob had a complexion richer in blood, striking blue eyes and dark brown hair. The room was separated into two sides. On either was a single bed. Jacob's duvet was an old Football kit - one he'd had for years- and his wall was plastered with pictures of girls and sporting heroes, not to mention a recent and growing collection of beermats and bottle caps.

Leo's bed was plain and blue and on the wall beside was a giant map of the world, with various quotes tacked around it. Directly over his headboard was a shelf, full beyond bursting point with books on every subject. 'That'll fall on your head one day, and then you won't be so smart,' Jacob had said to him when he'd first got their Dad to put it up. Leo took pleasure in this idea, as being injured by his books might have meant a few days to legitimately be off school. At that moment though, books were the last thing on his mind, and he crawled, exhausted, into his bed.

*

Leo was walking through a forest, one he knew but could not remember from where. The branch of every tree seemed to whisper to him, urging him on. The grass beneath his feet glowed vividly as he stepped on it. The birds above him sang melodically, picking up pace. He knew he had little time. He started running, green passing by in blurs, hopping streams and clearing rivers following the beat of the drum. He could see ahead, the path forked, the light obscured. He pressed faster, approaching a stone bridge. He had to get there. By any means necessary. He fell to his feet, tripped himself. Over the brow of the hill a great Lion had appeared, snarling, its mane coated in fresh blood. Leo struggled to stand. Fear had gripped him. The beast shook his foundations with a roar and readied itself to pounce. Every ounce of Leo's body seized up. He could still feel the Lion's roar vibrating through him.

*

The forest faded. Leo sat bolt upright. He could still hear the Lion. He was in his bed. Jacob, already dressed, was staring at him.
'It's h-happening again,' Jacob managed to say, shaking, and he bit his lip, determined not to cry. Their parents were fighting again, furiously this time, and without restraint. For a moment they sat, audience to madness, until,

CRACK

Jacob punched the nearest wall; his anger, frustration and sadness proving too much to deal with.
'Don't do that Jake! This is nothing to do with you OK?' said Leo, feeling sick. The sounds coming through to their room now bore no similarities to anything a Lion could produce and

were clearly the shrieking bombardment of allied enemies punctuated by the shattering of glass and the thumping of furniture.

'What am I supposed to do?! I hate this! Why are they doing this to each other?!' Jacob said, cradling his right hand in his left and breathing sharply in and out.

He was 16, more or less an adult, but Leo still felt responsible for the protection of his younger brother - regardless of how much he annoyed him. As he watched Jacob's head descend into his knees after a trebling in volume of the sounds coming from across the hall, all the pain, fear and inadequacy he'd been accumulating alone for countless years began to combine inside him. Every shout, every vibration through the floor made his arms tighten, his fists clench and his blood flow through him like lava over ice. Without stopping to think, he leaped to his feet.

'Where are you going?!' called Jacob

'Sorting this out!' shouted Leo and, his eyesight tunnelling, he flew across the landing on autopilot and shoved open the door. As the door receded a momentary silence fell over the room as his parents turned to face him, their bed - ordinarily made, pristine and with an icing of co-ordinated scatter cushions - was across the floor, duvet torn, mattress upturned and the pillows stained black. His mother was on the floor, seated bent kneed clutching on to the remains of the duvet, her eye make-up streaming down her face and vest straps falling to her lower arms. His father was standing, half naked in plain pyjama bottoms. On the carpet beneath them, where there weren't remnants of the bedspread, there were empty whisky bottles.

'WHAT IS GOING ON?! JACOB'S IN OUR ROOM SCARED HALF TO DEATH BECAUSE OF YOU TWO!!' Leo shouted with as much fury as he could, his voice cracking midway.

'N...n..nothing darling, go back to bed...... now; there's a good boy,' said Sandra, unnaturally maternal.

'You're drunk!! This place is a tip and you've probably wasted half of that booze on the floor!'

'Don't you dare speak to me like that,'

'Why not? It's the truth you old soak!' said Bob, his face as red as the scarlet walls. 'Look at you, dried up and pathetic. If I were him I wouldn't have any respect for you either.'

'SHUT UP!' shouted Leo. 'You're both as bad as each other! You need to get some help..... this has been going on for far too long!'

'Got it in one,'

'Bob... don't,' pleaded Sandra, 'please.'

'Got what?' asked Leo.

'Why shouldn't I eh? The boy's old enough to know. In fact he said so himself; this has been going on for far too long!'

'Old enough to know what?!'

'No, Bob.... please.... I've told you... it was just a mistake. Just one mistake. Never before nor since....'

'What mistake?!' Leo was getting desperate now. He felt like his blood was about to reverse its flow.

'Yeah, right, ok. I'll believe that one when I see it. Always out late, always secretive; never wanting me to see your phone calls! What's that all about eh?!'

'Dad, what are you talking about?'

'Hear this one, eh?' and Bob stumbled, half grinning but still keeping his eyes fixed on his wife, he pointed his thumb at Leo. 'Dad. DAD? At least we know for sure this one's not mine!! What happened?' He pushed his face as close to Sandra's as he could. 'Geezer at the orphanage decide to do you a two for one with some of his own donation?'

The room went cold. Leo was frozen solid. Nausea seemed to permeate every inch of his body, as piece by piece, his identity was plunged into verbal acid - leaving in its wake a bleached, hollow shell. The divine revolt he'd felt in his chest that had compelled him to enter the room had again transformed. He felt his heart tear out of his chest and rest against the open air.

'I...I'm ad..' the word would not come out. It couldn't be true. Sandra pushed herself up and ran for him, holding him tightly to her.

'I never meant for you to find out like this,' she wept.

'Or at all if you had your way. You and your 'perfect little family'. We're all just an illusion to keep the neighbours happy aren't we? All while you go gallivanting about town with all and sundry; up to god-knows-what.'

'No, Bob, no..... please.'

'Listen boy, you're better off without a mother like that, trust me.'

That was it. Leo had heard enough. His legs thawed and he pushed his mother away, slamming the door as he rushed through it.

'LOOK, JUST LOOK WHAT YOU'VE DONE NOW!!!' Sandra screamed.

'WHAT I'VE DONE? OH, IT'S NEVER YOUR FAULT IS IT MISS PERFECT?'

Leo's breathing was heavy and faltering, his whole body was tingling but he knew there was only one thing he could do. He ran back into his bedroom, where Jacob was standing and had clearly been pacing up and down, listening to every word. Leo threw himself to the floor and began scrabbling under his bed. 'Where is it?' he said. 'Come on, I'm sure I left it here.' He pushed an old copy of National Geographic to the side. 'Ah, got it!'

'What're you doing?' asked Jacob, his hand over his right eye, which was as puffy as the left, trying to conceal from his brother the fact that he'd been crying.

'I'm going, I'm sorry, I've got to get out of here,' said Leo and he pulled a plain white backpack out from his bed. He opened it with a click and found to his relief that it was still packed. A year previously, after a day in which he'd managed to be mugged, threatened and then come home to his parents drunkenly bickering; each blaming the other over whose fault it was that Leo couldn't stick up for himself, he'd grabbed his favourite bag and packed it with everything he'd need to survive on his own for a few days. Clothes change, compass, watch, torch and some money swiped from the till. He hadn't left that night, but decided to leave the pack there just in case.

'But where are you going?'

'Anywhere,' and he clicked the clasp shut again, threw the pack over his shoulder and began to look for his shoes.

'What about me?'

Those three words were like a dagger. They traced the letters of Jacob's name across Leo's surfaced heart. He stopped in his tracks.

'Look, I'm sorry, I'll come back for you. I promise. I just need to leave, ok?'

'Sure,' whispered Jacob, and didn't look in the slightest bit convinced.

'I'll email you, yeah? Keep a look out.'

'Mmm,' hummed Jacob, and he sat back on the edge of his bed.

'Come on, chin up. We'll both be out of here before we know it. Bye mate.'

But Jacob did not reply. He was staring at Leo's empty bed whilst the voices of their parents filled the room like a hurricane. Leo took one deep breath, in and out, and left the room.

He jumped the stairs in two, and for a second the idea to take some food, as provisions, crossed his mind. But he decided against it. Having anything more to do with them or from them made him feel sick. Crossing the shop floor he noticed again the nick, but did not look back. He unbolted the door and ran into the cold night air.

Luckily, the High street was deserted. Where previously the cars had provided the road with warmth and dynamism, the long and ancient street now seemed cold and dead. Devoid of feeling and meaning. The streetlamps turned Leo yellow. A connotation he did not want, he was desperate not to think about. 'You left him.' But he pressed on, running past his childhood haunts, the cobbles beneath his feet both smooth and awkward, the baker shop where he'd tasted his first gingerbread, the clock-tower on the side of the house which belonged to the maths tutor, the shop where he'd squandered his lunch money on sweets. Halfway up, a lifetime away from his shop, he veered left down an alleyway. Cut beneath two of the buildings on the main street, the qualities of the path, walled on three sides and then two; produced the most fantastic echo. Leo used to amuse himself by wandering this alley alone and calling out ridiculous words to hear them said to himself.

'You're gonna be fine,' he said loudly, slowing to a walk, satisfied the impending darkness would shroud his identity from all who knew him. Yet when the phrase returned to him he did not feel at ease, but more alone than ever. The double sound of his footsteps was in time with the pounding of his heart. Beyond the red-brick walls that rose on either side of him, home to climbing ivy and lichen just as eager to escape from the world as him, was a wooded copse, and further, in the darkness - the bounding dewy common.

   He marched from shadow to shadow, a guerrilla of his own fear, frightened that if anybody saw him the events of tonight would all be real. Five minutes' walk into the common he left the path, and ascended the closest hill. Here too, he'd been happy. He and Jacob had spent hours and days rolling - cigar shaped- to the bottom. All that was an illusion now. He had no brother. All the ties that had allowed him to feel safe if not secure felt now as if they had been marked in ink. Two signatures on paper, dissoluble in water and destroyed by delirium. He took the backpack off and pulled it into his chest, his eyes adjusting to the darkness. SNAP. A twig in the distance cracked and he wheeled round, suddenly aware of his surroundings. He was alone on an unlit common, in a village miles from the nearest town. As hard as he tried to look in the direction of the sound, all he could make out were the distant silhouettes of two massive conker trees, and any further sounds were drowned by them swaying in the wind. Metal sand falling onto a playground slide. His joints could not relax, but he turned and hugged his pack tighter. The sky above him was clear and the stars were out. Leo had once heard that Native Americans believed that the stars were the campfires of their ancestors, making their way to the afterlife. Of course, he knew the truth. But he preferred the belief and it gave him solace, imagining thousands of other wanderers in the dark; not knowing where to go or when they would find their next destination, all looking down at him with a knowing smile. They had been on this plane before.

   A lone car rounded the bend into the village, its lights shooting stars within the common sky. The purr of the engine and the crackle of the wheels on the asphalt roused Leo's attention long before the headlights. At a steady pace it traversed the road which cut through the wide open space, a veteran soldier's war-wound, unsightly but necessary for recollection. The closer it came to the mound where Leo was sat, the more he could make out its shape. Plain, large and black. A streamlined 4x4. At the point of the road opposite the mound it slowed, click by click on asphalt, to a stop. Leo's heart raced. It was god knows what time in the morning and someone had decided to stop here. He saw a movement through the windscreen, but could not be certain of what lay behind. Too scared even to breathe he waited.

SNAP

Another twig behind Leo had met its end and as he looked over his shoulder instinctively, the 4x4 drove off at considerable speed down the road -towards the High Street.
'Calm down, they've obviously lost an animal,' Leo said to himself and, with a shudder, tugged down at his sleeves and looked at the stars once more.
At first he thought he was imagining it. Tiny lights had begun to dance across the sky above him. He blinked hard to clear his eyes, and yet, there they were still. Gentle flickers at first, growing into elegant flashes of violet, azure blue and leaf green. Oranges and purples collided and waltzed across the common and then they filled the sky. In the High Street, a distant alarm sounded, followed by others from the four corners of the village. Leo gazed, transfixed and bewildered, a grin smeared across his face and his mind clear.
'This is!!Ha, haha,' he said to no one.
'Hahahahaha...........Oww!! Itttthhhh',' he winced, razorblades were slicing his wrist, his right hand was being dipped in hydrochloric over and over. The fire from the pain met his eyes and they stung, a light appeared in front of him.
'AHHHHHHHHHHHHH!!!! ARRRGGGGGGHHHHH.....WHAT IS..... AHHHHHH!!!!!' the pain overtook him and he subsided to darkness.

Found & Lost

In a grand office, deep in Central London, the heavy wooden door creaked open.

'Sir?' said a Junior Official, barely audible over the hum of the ceiling fans that churned the otherwise stale air.

'Yes?' replied a genial voice from the other side of the room; a broad figure seated behind an ornate wooden desk.

'They have him.'

The man behind the desk immediately closed his laptop, raised his eyes to the Junior and sank back into his seat.

'See to it that all the usual procedures are followed...... as well as my previous orders.'

'Yes Sir.'

'I cannot stress enough the importance of this,' he paused, leaned forward to place his elbow on the desk and stroked his lips.

'Nor what will befall any who fail.'

'Absolutely, Sir.'

'Thank you, Dean.'

'Sir,' said the official, and left, closing the door behind him.

A grimace spread across the man's face, contorting the scar that ran vertically from above his left temple to his chin. He ran his fingers through his jet black hair and then, with the same hand, pulled open a drawer in the desk. He pulled out a large, leather-bound book and dropped it, with a thump, beside his laptop. He stroked the spine, and sighed. He was about to redeem himself. His eyes traced the beaten cover, the pockmarked leather still shining beneath the warm lighting as if it were new. He let them linger on the emblem marked in gold in the centre of the cover. A rearing unicorn that was chained to three golden bars and being whipped by a disembodied fist.

He breathed in deeply, squaring his shoulders, and opened the book.

*

   A sudden shake roused Leo from sleep. He opened his eyes to what at first appeared to be absolute darkness. He remembered how his eyes had begun to burn last night and became frightened he might be blind. 'Not that, please.... anything but that' he thought. But slowly, as the sleep washed from his eyes, he began to make out two slits of light on the same level as what he was sitting on. 'Where the hell am I!?' he thought as his wrist began to tingle and he recalled the pain he'd felt. 'I must've blacked out' His head felt fuzzy, and his skull made of steel. Whilst he squinted to see more of his surroundings he was suddenly thrown onto his back and became aware of the chug-chugging of an engine. 'I'm in a van. And the back of one at that'. If only he could see what was around him, he might be able to look for a way out. Then it came to him. Backpack. He'd packed a torch in with his other equipment. But where was it? He began feeling around him in the darkness, groping like a beggar eager for coins.' Wood. Floor. Smooth, Still wood: wall'. His hand clenched something soft, quite pleasant but slightly warm. It was almost furry. Definitely not his backpack.
   'Ah, gotcha!' he whispered as he fumbled behind him. Clumsily pulling it in front of him, he clicked open the clasp and dug inside. 'The books were a bad idea,' he thought and his stomach twinged as he remembered passing up the food. 'Brilliant,' his hand found the torch, pressed down on the button and he pulled it out of the bag to illuminate the space.
   'Oh. My...' he said, resisting the urge to gag from the smell his movement had stirred up and swallowed down hard. On the high sides of the van were wooden shelves and metal hooks supporting three different sized saws, a shovel, two cans of liquid bearing a yellow 'toxic' label and finally, closest to the doors, which were splattered with dried mud - two shotguns, a pistol, and a dagger. The floor of the van was stained by a liquid, black by torchlight and looked like it had been dragged across the length of the compartment to the

doors. Leo's eyes drank in the torture chamber and he began to shiver. Then the torchlight descended on what was next to him, resting on the floor. There, eyes glinting like glass marbles and tongue lolling with abandon, lay the severed head of a stag. Dried blood was matted into its fur. Leo realised with disgust how the soft thing he'd touched earlier must have been the neck of this once-noble beast. He turned the torch towards himself and found that he was covered in its blood. 'What the!' He was repulsed and tried to stand, but another bump in the road threw him back to the floor and winded him. The van started to climb, he could feel it urging upwards and he began to slide towards the doors. He wasn't going to stick around one more second to find out where this abattoir on wheels was headed. Grabbing his bag he launched himself at the doors. He pushed the handle hard, but it was no use. It wouldn't budge.

'COME ON,' he breathed and as he rested his head on the door, distraught, his eyes found the pistol. He shoved the torch in his mouth, reached for the weapon and without thinking, aimed directly at the handle and fired. Three shots exploded into the metal, weakening them beyond doubt. Knowing he would've been heard, he tossed the pistol aside, threw down the torch, took a few steps back and ran with everything he had. His pain, his parents' admittance, his desertion solidified and became an instrument of destruction and this door was condemned. His shoulder met the metal.

BANG

He rolled out of the van and on to the road, his body free-falling at so many miles per hour. He felt like he was in the centre of a tornado, unsure which way was up but knowing that every way was hurt. Behind him the van had stopped, and a black figure had got out of the driver's side. Leo came to a halt beside a metal guard and felt his entire body ache. A warmth cascading down his eyebrow told him he'd been cut. But now all he had to do was run. He heaved himself up and fell almost immediately back down.

'COME.... ON!....' he shouted at himself. And he ran, thinking only of Jacob; how he had to get back to him, to save him. He was there still, picking up the pieces and Leo had left. Hopping over the numerous stones so as not to trip, he headed towards the forest in front of him - gunshots flying above his head. His breathing had become sharp and erratic, his adrenalin pumping like never before. He kept running. For miles he ran, never stopping to check behind him until eventually he fell, exhausted, to the ground. What the hell was going on? He was only a Shopkeeper's son, a village boy whose most interesting exploit was seeing the Coliseum in Rome earlier that year. What did anybody want from him?

The wind strained through the trees and over them a hawk circled, tracking a mouse that had eluded it for hours. Its alpha eyesight had locked on from the start but the mouse had escape-holes too readily available. Now, with its nearest exit blocked by a human that wouldn't be moving for some time, it was doomed. The hunger that drove the hawk would soon be satisfied, and it would move on to its next victim - a brother, or sister of the last perhaps.

Slumped beneath a pine tree, Leo sat for hours; jumping at every minor noise. In the early hours of the morning his body told him to sleep but he could not. He thought he would be found. Shot. Killed. Eventually though, with his bag supporting his back, he drifted off into a fitful, uneasy sleep.

*

'Hey, guys! Get over here! Quickly!' called a Scottish accent.

'What? Found more Owl-pellets again?' said another and three voices laughed simultaneously.

'No, this is serious, just come!'

Rounding the corner from where their view had been obscured, three people - two guys and a girl - saw their friend on her knees, crouching beside a pale, bloodied boy.

'Definitely not anything animal-related,' said the tallest boy and he exchanged concerned looks with the others. 'Come on,' and they all quickened their pace.

'What do you think's happened to him?' said the girl with

long brown hair, keeping her distance.

'Looks like someone's jumped him,' offered the shorter of the two boys.

'But we're in the middle of nowhere,' said the other.

'*We're* here.'

'True.'

'He looks about our age.... underneath all that blood... is he breathing?' asked the girl.

'Yeah, I've been watching his chest,' said the girl who was next to him, and she raised her hand to Leo's mouth, 'and... yep, my hand's warm.'

'Well that's something at least.'

'Have you tried to wake him?' asked the taller boy, stepping closer to the tree beneath which Leo was resting.

'N..not yet, no,' said the girl, tucking her red hair behind her ear.

'Don't you think we should? It doesn't look like he's got anything broken. A couple of cuts and bruises maybe..'

'Ok... here we go,' and she shifted her weight from knee to knee, placed her hand lightly on his shoulder and said loudly: 'Hello! Hello, Can you hear me?' She gently shook Leo and his head moved back and forth. 'Hello.. wake up.'

Leo's eyes opened slowly at first, and then widened, taking his eyebrows with them. He tried to push back, jumping, but the tree blocked his way and he fell to his side.

'Hey! No, it's ok! We're not gonna hurt you!' said the girl that was bent down beside him. She had sleek, red hair that fell to her waist, one side tucked behind her ear. Her eyes were green and three freckles kissed the tops of either cheek. She wore an ivy jumper, and acidwash jeans beneath. As much as he tried he couldn't look away.

'You alright there buddy?' said a tall, mousey boy from behind her. 'You look like you've been through a war'.

Something like that.

'Yeah, yeah I'm fine thanks.... er.. ' said Leo, and he tried to stand up, 'Where....where am I?'

The groups' face morphed from concern to confusion before his eyes.

'You don't know where you are?' said another girl, standing furthest away from Leo, but steadily edging closer.

'No.. I mean, last thing I knew I was in Hertfordshire.' His head was really starting to hurt now.

'You're a long way from Hertfordshire, pal,' said a shorter, blonde boy.

Leo's face screwed up in despair. 'You...what?'

'We're in Scotland. The Highlands to be precise. And a remote part at that,' said the redhead's smooth voice.

How? What? There was no way this could be happening. Leo had never set foot inside of Scotland. In fact he'd never even seen the border.

'What's the last thing that you remember?' asked the redhead, trying to comprehend the look on Leo's face.

Leo looked around at them. He couldn't tell them about seeing the Northern Lights in Middle England and getting a pain in his hand that caused him to black out , then waking up in a van next to a mutilated deer and .. oh wait.. been shot at. They'd think he was even more insane than they already did. And they seemed like decent people. Best to measure out the truth.

'I'd run away from home. I'd had an argument, and left. Yesterday was my birthday and-'

'Your birthday!?'

'Yeah,'

'What age were you?'

'Eighteen.'

'Happy Birthday,' said the group in unison.

'Er, thanks, well.. yeah, I'd had an argument, ran away from home and... that's the last I remember.'

'D'ya wanna know what I think?' said the tall boy.

'What?'

'I reckon, you're an adult now... and you're not wanting to go home, right?'

'Well, no, but..'

'Then, you can come with us. We're on a road trip around, and you need cleaning up anyway. That alright guys?'

There was silence, the other three had been staring at the blood on Leo's hoody and the unusual colour of his eyes.

'GUYS?' The silence broke.

'Oh....Yeah,'

'Yeah, of course.'

'Definitely.'

'Then it's settled,' said the taller guy triumphantly, and strode across to Leo, arm outstretched, 'I'm Blake.' Leo took his hand and shook it and a smile spread across Blake's face. His handshake was firm and matched his athletic build. Blake then pointed to the others.

'That's Alec,' The shorter, blonde boy nodded back.

'Alrigh'?'

'Mercia.'

The girl with brown hair waved and said 'Hiya.'

'and finally..'

'Isla,' said the flame-haired girl, standing up and extending her hand. 'Pleased to meet you...?'

'Leo... I'm Leo.'

'Sure about that?' Isla teased.

'Yeah, nothing else, but I'm certain of that,' and he laughed.

'Come on then man, let's get you back to the car -you got a change of clothes in.... there?' said Blake pointing to Leo's backpack.

'Yeah, somewhere,' replied Leo a little sheepishly, having realised seconds before that his favourite backpack, once as white as snow, now looked like a murder scene. Two large brown handprints had been left either side of the pack, and one on top. 'Dried deer blood,' he thought, 'Nice...'

'Excellent, come on then, car's just beyond this wood,' and Blake dropped his voice to a mock whisper, 'don't tell anyone - we took it off road.'

'I won't,' said Leo.

The four of them made their way through the widely spaced trees, trying to keep their balance on the carpet of moss which had rolled out before them. VIPs to a limousine. Not quite.

'Watch the Old Man's beard!' screeched Isla as she leapt gleefully over a rock.

'I would, but it pains me to look at you for too long,' quipped Alec, glancing to an appreciative Blake.

'Oh Ha-Ha. Get back to me when you can actually grow a beard Al.'

'Can't I just borrow some of yours?'

'What's Old Man's Beard?' asked Mercia reproachfully.

'That shadow on Isla's face.'

'Yes, thank you Ein-Swine. Mercy, it's that bright green moss. Looks a little bit like candy floss. On the floor and the trees. Can you see it?'

'Errr,' said Mercia. At this Isla stretched up and pulled some Old Man's beard from a tree.

'Look!' said Isla and held her hand out to Mercia's face; who screamed.

'AHHH, Get your snot AWAY from me!'

'It's not... It grows where-ever the air is pure. Can't tolerate pollution,' said Isla whilst Mercia cowered behind Blake. 'Though what it's doing alive round here with you lot is another matter!'

'Haha, ignore them Iz. They're winding you up,' said Blake.

'Mmm, well.'

'That reminds me..'

'What?'

'Do you have a spare razor? I could do with a shave.'

'Arrrrrgh!!!! I give up!!!' and she sped infront of them to the car. When they caught up, she was tapping her fingers on the roof, face like thunder.

'And don't you dare think for one second that I'm driving! Bloody lot....' and she half-grinned.

Everyone laughed, even Leo to his surprise. One by one they filed in to the car, all except Leo and Blake. Leo had hesitated before getting in, throwing a disapproving look at his clothes.

'Don't worry about it mate. It's my car, just get in and we'll get you changed and cleaned up at the next petrol station,' said Blake.

'You sure?'

'100%. Get in,' and he climbed into the driver's seat.

Leo got in, glad to have the window seat. However, sat next to Isla he felt incredibly awkward. He was disgusted with his attire and felt eagles circling within his stomach. He wondered whether there would be food wherever it was they were going, but didn't mention a word to the others. He daren't even move. One flinch and Isla might have backed away from him, stealing the comfort he felt at his side. As they accelerated faster towards a road, the radio came on with a crackle, and Blake turned the dial almost all the way up. Bon Jovi -Instant sing-a-long.

Whilst the others exercised their vocal cords, Leo sat in silence, staring at the vast expanse beyond the window, and was glad he was there, cocooned inside a social capsule. Albeit an insanely fresh one. Why did it feel like Isla was staring at him? This made him even more uncomfortable. 'She thinks I'm a mass murderer. I'm covered in blood head to toe and they're gonna take me to the police station.' he thought.

'Are you wearing contacts?' came Isla's smooth voice from the left, sailing over the bold harmonies with ease.

Leo turned to look at her. 'No, why?' In reality, he was humouring her. He'd been asked the same questions over and over. It annoyed him for a while, made him wonder how people could be so ignorant, but in the end; he resolved that people are, by and large, just curious. Hyper curious. And sometimes stupid. But this one wasn't. So he played the fool.

'You've just got...... I mean. They're really pretty.'

'Pretty? Er.. thanks.'

'No, I mean, I mean mesmerising. Like I could get lost in them,' Leo felt his eyes burn, 'And I swear they just got lighter!'

'Oh, maybe? Thanks.'

'Do you know why they're like that?'

'Not really, Doctors always told me it was genetic. A defect or mutation of some sort. They're not too sure either.'

'Interesting.'

'Interesting?'

'Yeah, I mean, interesting to know that there are still some things we can't be sure of, or know the ins and outs of in today's world. Gives me hope.'

'Really? You like to know that we can't know everything?'

'Yeah, I guess. I just think that there are things that we can't - that we shouldn't - understand.'

Leo thought of the Atomic Bomb and the creation of Chimeras and decided that Isla had a point.

'What do you think?' she asked, pushing her hair behind her ears.

'Oh, I, you know,' Leo didn't really understand how he was

still able to think with the last 48 hours he'd had, let alone articulate those thoughts to a stunningly beautiful girl, pressed up against him in a car. 'I guess I agree with you. But there are still some things I'd like to know.'

'Like what?'

'The usual. Why we're here, is there an afterlife? Why is there so much suffering? Etc.'

'And what if we did know the answers to those questions?'

'Then life would be.....'

'Meaningless. No point of planning for tomorrow because you'd know what those tomorrows would ultimately lead to.'

'Well, no, I think-'

'WAHEY! Nerds! Back-seat, chill down please, we've now arrived at Service Station 103, please remain in your seats and keep your belts fastened until the vehicle stops moving, I'd like to say on behalf of my self and my vintage Ford Fiesta, thank you for flying with Highland Air and a safe journey to the toilet!' said Blake, in his mock-pilot best, received to widespread laughter.

'Got to peeeeee!' said Mercia, slamming the door behind her as she ran across the forecourt.

'Aye, me too, getting out Al?' said Isla.

'Aye.'

'See you back here in ten, Leo, ok? I think Blake's gonna top up, aren't you?'

'Yeah,' said Blake heading to the back of the car.

'Ok.'

'Toilets are in the back - right hand corner,' and she left.

Leo waited a moment, pulling his pack towards him and watching the other drivers on the forecourt. One in the car opposite had placed the nozzle back and started pulling faces through the back window to his son, who beamed back at him in hysterics - a facial embodiment of the absent sun. When Leo was absolutely certain that the court was clear, or at least that everyone was busy with themselves, he left the car and half-jogged to the shop. The two men behind the counter were deep in conversation and they gave Leo just a fleeting look. Leo considered himself to be incredibly lucky. His angelic appearance had always prevented people from being suspicious of him. He'd once stolen a chocolate bar from the shop across the road from him, and later, racked with guilt, when he tried to return it - the patron refused to believe he'd stolen anything 'You must've bought it somewhere else and forgotten love, go on now' and ushered him out of the shop. Of course, he ate up the bar greedily, but those hours of menacing guilt had taught him never to try the perfect crime again.

The toilets were actually, for the gents at least, a single cubicle with a lock, basin and a mirror. They looked as if they hadn't been cleaned for a long while and smelt overwhelmingly of ammonia. The back of the door had been marked by years of graffiti, painted over and then added to again. The most prominent being a now-black carving in letters 4 inches high: 'ALBA' . Unwilling to put anything but his shoes on the floor, Leo balanced his bag on the cistern of the toilet and turned to face the mirror. He looked horrific. His own blood stained his face and had in places turned black as it dried. Flecks of the road, dust and asphalt had stuck within the trail of blood down the left side of his face, and the right was grazed and brown. His clothes were ripped in many places, and worn down to the skin in others. Thick patches the shape of fried eggs clung to his hoody like moist black badges. 'A Scouts commendation for survival,' he thought. He shook his head, and began to undress, slowly, as every movement sent a stinging pain through to his core.

He clenched his teeth as the fabric unstuck itself from his wounds, and dragged, bristling over his milken skin. Every last piece he threw into the small plastic bin. There was no way they could be rescued. Leaning over the basin, he washed the blood from his face; little by little exposing more of the boy behind the mask. He had the strangest feeling that he'd been trick-or-treating and that last night was some gharish Hallowe'en nightmare caused by sugar-overload, but no costume requires the use of your own blood and when his stomach growled his fantasies were put entirely to rest.

Surveying his now clean visage in the mirror, he felt a little better. He touched the deep cut above his left eyebrow and recoiled, breathing through his teeth. 'That one's gonna scar.'

'Now you're even less good looking than me!' He imagined his brother saying to him sarcastically. He bit his tongue and moved towards his bag, and opened it with one hand.

'I really should learn how to pack properly,' he murmured to himself as he rifled through the bag that by now was almost overflowing and in no kind of order. He pulled out a thick woollen jumper, dark blue with white-knitted snowflakes across the chest and quickly put it on, aware that he said he'd only be ten minutes and he still needed to get food. As he grabbed a pair of jeans and tugged hard to unleash them from the stranglehold of the other items inside, he saw something brown fly out of the bag. Pulling on his jeans, he wrinkled up his face and stared hard at the envelope that had landed beneath the sink. He closed his bag and crouched down, leaning into the wall. The envelope had managed to lodge itself between the ceramic and the yellowing wall. When he'd gotten a grip on it, he pulled it towards him and held it in both hands.

Leo

How could this possibly have come to be in his bag? He racked his brains to try and remember if it was something sentimental, something his Granddad had given him before he'd passed away and he couldn't bear to be without. Something important should he ever leave home, but it was no use. Not once did the idea ever cross his mind to take anything sentimental. As far as he was concerned, if he left, anything that tied him to that place stayed and dissolved. Yet, here he was, holding an envelope, addressed to him when no one else knew about the backpack. Unable to control himself any longer, he tore it open and pulled out a folded piece of pre-lined paper.

Aloysius Building,
Pére David's Orphanage,
Fort Augustus.
PH32 7NU
A2.

Within the forests and beneath the lochs,
the truth is painted for all to see.

*When her sweet light shines on the rocks,
you'll find who you were meant to be.*

*Seek out the wave, the beach and sky,
and you'll find those who'd lost all hope.
They live in numbers, are forced to die,
Leo, cut your Mother's noose and rope.*

*The less you look, the more you'll find.
With luck we'll leave these days behind.*

*Yours,
      St. Humility.*

   Leo pushed himself upwards sharply.
   'OUCH!!' With full attention on the letter, he'd smacked straight into the hard ceramic basin above. Smarting, he paced, re-reading the letter several times before grabbing his bag and heading out the door, through the shop and towards the car. When came next to its red and rusty hull, he saw that the windows had steamed up with their breath. 'God I hope they haven't been waiting ages'. He opened the door, letter still clasped in his hand and climbed in.
   'Alright mate? We thought you'd fallen in!' came Blake's voice from the front.
   'Ahh, you look miles better,' said Mercia, straining round to see him.
   'Don't look like you're on the Most Wanted list anymore,' said Alec, nodding to Leo.
   'Haha, yeah, cheers, sorry I took so long, I-'
   'What's that?' Isla interrupted, gesturing to the now well creased letter in Leo's hand.
   'Oh... it's... something I found in my backpack. Didn't put it in there, don't know who it's from.'
   'That looks like an address at the top.'
   'Yeah, it's an orphanage somewhere... Scotland, actually. Not sure if it exists.'
   'Orphanage?' said Alec.
   'Yeah, well... funny thing is, that's one of the reasons I ran away from home last night.'

'What is?' said Mercia.
'Oh come off it babe,' said Blake.
'No, really, what?'
'The lad just told you he's found the address of an orphanage Merse,' said Alec, his tone impatient.
'Yeah?'
'Oh for crying out loud.'
'Look, it's ok. I found out I was adopted last night... two nights ago actually.. and now I've found an address to an orphanage in a backpack that I was pretty sure no one else knew about,' said Leo, feeling himself go numb.

The car went silent. Across the forecourt a man in a high-visibility waistcoat paid an old woman at a mobile canteen for a cup of coffee, and walked off.

'Sorry,' said Mercia, blushing.
'It's-'
'Well you know what this means guys!' said Blake, his voice rising cheerfully.
'What?'
'Another destination for the trip!' and he tooted the horn. 'Woo Woo!'
'Isn't our itinerary a bit packed as it is?' queried Alec and the other three Scots glowered at him. 'Or not. Actually, yeah, we've got plenty of time.'
'Absolutely!' said Isla and she playfully squeezed Leo's knee. 'So... to...' and she leaned across him to see the letter more clearly. Leo could smell her hair. Cinammon and Vanilla. He quickly looked out of the window. 'Fort Augustus it is then!'
'Brilliant, that's not out of our way at all,' exclaimed Blake. 'We wanted to go Nessie hunting anyway. That's where Fort Augustus is. On the shore of the Bonnie Black Lochhhhh.' They all laughed.
'Right, off we go then,' and he turned the key in the ignition. 'Sod the maps Mercy, this is an ADVENTURE!' he said as his girlfriend was fumbling in the glove compartment.
'I was just getting my iPod. It might be an adventure, but we need a soundtrack eh?'
'Please don't put on any of your electro stuff. I've got enough of a headache sitting next to the Professor back

here,' said Alec with a feint grin that Blake returned.

'No go on, please do. Let's inflict some aural pain on this wind-up merchant,' said Isla and she jabbed Alec in the ribs with her elbow.

'Alright! Alright!' said Alec. 'I back down, Supreme Brain of the Entire Universe.' She jabbed again. 'Ow! But, come on, please, let's just have some decent music.'

'Done,' said Mercia and she turned the dial up three notches.

A symphony of bagpipes and harps filled the car, building steadily with some percussion to a minor crescendo and then a female vocalist started screeching in a language Leo didn't understand.

'What the HELL is this!?' shouted Alec over the racket.

'Scottish music, for our southern friend back there. Consider it an introduction to Alba.'

'Mate, I like a bagpipe as much as the next man but this is hideous. If I were him I'd turn straight back round and run for the border,' said Alec, covering his ears, and everybody laughed.

'Aye alright then,' said Mercia and the track switched in a second to an Indie number by a popular Scottish band.

'Are you hungry?' Isla asked Leo.

'Starving,' replied Alec.

'I wasn't asking you.' She bent down to a thin plastic bag she had tucked between her legs. 'Here!' she chucked a cereal bar at Alec, 'and these are for you,' she said, passing two different flavours of bar to Leo.

'Didn't know which one you'd like, eat the one you prefer first.' Her eyes sparkled.

'Excellent, thanks!' said Leo, feeling the blood rush to his cheeks. He thought eating might get rid of the nausea.

She then gave one each to the front-seaters and for a while the entire car was content, munching on their snacks, awestruck by the marvellous scenery which passed them in abundance. For Leo the silence allowed his mind to wander, the lyrics of the music pulling at his strings. It should have been obvious to him, the adoption, he was never like his family. They prized the glory of success and the material benefits it brought. As children, both Leo and Jacob were plied with mountains of presents; each had one side of a tree that was erected in their room, and on the mantelpiece hung a stocking for them both, overflowing with the saccharine glitter of western yule. Whilst Jacob eagerly tore through his gifts, counting the number at the end and comparing it with Leos', Leo opened them all slowly and in succession; appreciating each and every one. Often he would leave the biggest of them all 'til last, and after opening it, would let Jacob have the first go - finding pure bliss in the endless possibilities of a box that size. To Leo it was a castle, a den, a ship sailing across the pale blue living room carpet to foreign climes. When the last of their presents had been opened and his mum came to collect the wrapping paper for the bin, Leo would protest.

'But what can you do with it now?' she would say and Leo could not reply. He was too young to offer a suggestion, but thought it wrong nonetheless. That glimmer which could transform the mundane, the brittle plastic or mass-produced video into an excruciating mystery, a catalyst of excitement - deserved a better home than the pitch black void of the kitchen bin. Still, they'd kept him safe, kept him warm and shown him love. A ruthless, selfish love in the case of his parents, too wrapped up in themselves to realise the damage they were doing to their children, maybe. But it was love still. Those ties had now been shattered. Every second of his life had been a lie and he was a stranger even to himself. When the chorus of an 80's number hit, his eyes began to well up.

CLICK

Off went the iPod.
   'Right, I think that looks like an interesting little pit-stop, don't you?' Blake said, pointing out of the car's left windows, where below them in the distance stood the ruins of a castle, nestled beside a loch and in full view of the towering mountains.
   Leo cleared his throat loudly and let his jaw drop slightly.
   'D'you,' he said, 'd'you get many of those up here?'
   'Many of what?' said Mercia.
   'Castles.'

'Nah,' said Alec.
'Oh.'
'Only about a thousand or more,' laughed Alec.
'This is gonna be pretty bumpy guys, sorry,' said Blake as he pulled into a tiny lay-by. The car shuddered and shook everyone like beans in a maraca.
'Woah!' shouted Isla.
'I did warn ye,' said Blake.
'You said bumpy. Not factor seven earthquake!'
At last, the car came to a halt with a satisfying grind of the handbrake.
'Meh,' said Blake, and he jumped out of the car followed slowly by the others.
'Right; whoever gets there first is the King!'
'King!?' said Mercia with one eyebrow raised.
'Okay, or Queen, Monarch eh? Whoever gets there first is the ruler of the bonnie Castle.'
'You're on,' said Alec stretching off.
'Three!' called Blake, the wind blowing through his hair.
'Two!' said Isla as she bounced on the spot.
'One!' shouted Alec and they all readied themselves.
'Goooooooooooooooooooooo!!' finished Mercia and they launched themselves, bounding down the hill at full pace.
Leo, who was slow off the mark, left later than the others, feeling naked without his pack. 'This is....' he thought at first as he stumbled down the hill, but then, gaining speed and feeling the pure air rush through him, his eyes on the Castle before them, 'brilliant!!' . His feet touched the ground for no more than a second each time, and he was soon cantering alongside Alec, who was panting hard. He put his head down, and feeling a rush that spread outwards from his stomach his speed increased. Before long he'd surpassed the girls, who had taken to turning round - running backwards- and taunting Alec. Only Blake remained infront of him and he could feel that with one deep breath and one last push he could overtake even him. His cheeks burned with the slashes of the wind as he stared at Blake's broad shoulders, dipped like a landing concorde and decided, that maybe this time, it was better to concede defeat. 'I'm the guest here. Not the friend. Not the King' and he slowed.

'Yeaaaaaaaaaaaah!!' screamed Blake as he slammed into the wall of the Castle.

'I'm..........the........King!' he said between deep breaths.

Leo slowed to a walking pace, and touched the Castle, His hand felt like it was being rubbed against sandpaper.

'And you, you sir, are my Lord,' said Blake, with a salute to Leo, who bowed in deference.

'And my Damsels! My Queen...' and he held his arms out as though he were in the stocks, Mercia climbed beneath one.

'And her Lady-in-waiting!' Isla climbed beneath the other.

'And this.... this would be our court Jester!' he said, to all round laughter as Alec wheezily pigeon stepped his way to the wall.

'Aye.....Ok..... So I'm a little...... Unfit,' Alec stuttered as if every word caused him discomfort.

'A little?' said Mercia, 'You look like you're about to keel over...'

'Ch... I'm fine,'

'Too many greasy spoons and late nights that is mate,' said Blake

'So we can rule out that as a career path for you then,' said Isla, her tone dry.

'What's that?'

'Anything that involves moving,' she said, the freckles on her cheeks raising. 'Maybe we should have strapped a fry-up to Blake's back, then he would've run.'

'Nah. I'm not keen on fast food.'

'Touché!' called Blake, flashing his teeth in a wide smile.

'How old do you reckon this is?' asked Isla, who had released herself from Blake's arms and was standing a few feet away from them, staring upwards at the bleak ruins.

Decay had worn away at the edges of the once chiselled exterior, the rouge moss climbing far enough up the walls to make it seem as if the entire building had been hurled up from the ground - a living, breathing monument. These ravages, however, had done nothing to reduce its power and Leo, walking beside Isla, gazed at the slit-like windows and could almost hear the clashing of broadswords and zooming of arrows.

'Few hundred years?' called Mercia, from within the old

courtyard, 'Or more.'

'What? Where are you Merse?' said Isla, hopelessly spinning on the spot.

'I went round the back, there's a door... or... well... there was a door. More of a gap now. There's a courtyard.'

Leo and Isla continued on round the outer walls of the Castle, eager to see what Mercia had found, but just as intrigued with where they were. Leo tried his hardest to keep his eyes on the stonework, to imagine how long it must have taken the builders to construct this place in an age before cranes - but that red hair would not go away.

Towards the far end of the outer wall they came to a halt. Before them a thin part of the Loch cut across their path.

'Uh oh,' said Isla.

'Yeah... we'll have to go back round,' replied Leo, and he turned, one hand leaning on the Castle wall.

THUD

Leo spun on his heel and caught Isla climbing up from her knees, her light jeans now stained with mud.

'Come on, now you!' she called whilst pulling a water bottle from her tye-dye shoulder bag.

'Err,' Leo looked deep and hard at the black water, his eyes flickering from precipice to precipice, assessing the distance. He was awful at long-jump at school.

'Come on!! It's not that hard really. I saw you jump further than that when we ran down the hill!' 'Yeah, but that was on soft mossy terrain. Not icy black waters of death.'

'Can I have some of that first?' Leo asked, nodding at the water bottle in her hand.

'Sure,' she said, tucked her hair behind her ears and tightened the lid of the bottle. 'Just don't drop it ok?'

'Done,' said Leo. And she launched the bottle towards him like a cricket ball. With a gentle clap it landed in Leo's hands. Inhaling deeply, he unscrewed the lid, took three long gulps and then chucked it back the same way it had come.

'Okay, here goes,' said Leo, and he took three paces backwards, fixed his eyes on the opposite side, and ran. 'I'm gonna make it,' he told himself.

'AHHHHHHH!' Isla screamed, and its shrill pitch sunk into the depths of Leo's skull.

A small head had popped up above the water that lay between them, its dark eyes scanning Isla, before turning to face Leo. Its mouth opened and closed slightly, revealing a pink interior and sharp, vicious teeth.

SPLASH

Leo, distracted by Isla's scream and the appearance of the head, had fallen short of the bank. Half his body lay splayed beneath Isla, the other drowned in the loch.

'Here!' shouted Isla and she held her grasped Leo's arm beyond the elbow. She tugged and Leo tried to get a foothold, desperate to be on dry land.

'Just....nearly,' but he flailed, the water splashing them both. Finally, his foot found a strong foundation and with the combined force of Isla's pull and Leo's push, they fell into a dripping heap on the bank. Within seconds, they parted, and Leo sat up, wiped the water from his forehead and stared into the Loch.

'S....sorry about that,' said Isla as she stood.

'What was it?' Leo said, his head swirling.

'An otter.'

'An otter?'

'Yeah, we get loads of them up here.'

'So why the scream?' Leo turned to face her.

'It surprised me,' she said, her face like rhubarb.

'It....?' began Leo, but it was too much, and he collapsed onto his back in hysterics.

'It's not funny!........ it could have been anything!'

When was she going to stop. The fire was burning fiercely enough. She didnt need to add more fuel. Leo could barely stop laughing, but he managed to stutter:

'Like.... a branch... or a bird.... or a leaf!'

'Otters can be pretty dangerous you know.'

Leo's laughter intensified, became louder. A smile broke across Isla's face. Cautiously at first, like a duck taking bread.

And then she too started laughing, shaking her head as she watched Leo rolling on the floor. She'd swallowed the loaf.

*

'Where've you two been?'
Leo and Isla had found the entrance to the courtyard, still in fits of laughter - unaware of anyone around them, and were ambling, slowly, towards the centre.
'Hello!...We heard a scream,' said Alec in a harsh tone and their faces fell.
'Sorry.. we got abit... stuck.. and an otter scared me.'
'Right.'
'Look Al' I'm sorry ok?'
'Yeah, cool, we're going in a minute.' He turned his back on them, and started walking towards Mercia, who was looking at something high up on the back wall.
Leo waited until he was out of earshot and then asked 'Blimey... What's wrong with him?'
'Oh, nothing, just concerned I guess... we were gone a while,' said Isla quietly, shifting her weight from foot to foot and flicking her hair out of her face.
Leo didn't buy it, personally. All they'd been doing was having a laugh, having fun. Wasn't that what they were supposed to be doing? He wondered if perhaps there was something he wasn't being told, maybe they really were suspicious of him and him spending any time alone with one of their number was as dangerous leaving them in a cage with a wild animal.
'Yeah.'
'Anyway, let's go see what they're looking at.... if we're going in a minute we should at least check out the rest of the place,' she said as she pulled at the bobbles on her damp jumper, looking Leo up and down. 'Plus, the walking will help dry you out.'
She had a point, he was drenched. If it wasn't summer he'd have been in serious trouble, but as it was, the damp was only a minor irritation. After all, he'd been covered in worse things that day.
As they made their way towards the others, the far wall

came into sharp focus. Carved on a single, large slab a foot above their heads was a coat of arms. Though it had been battered and beaten by centuries of weather, the details remained discernible. On the shield was a single circle, its outline thick and its radius almost as large as the shield itself. The supporters on either side of the shield were rampant wolves; each sporting a crown. Having grown up surrounded by heraldry none of this surprised Leo at all. He knew that different aristocratic families had vastly different coats of arms, and save for the layout, each one unique and personal to them. What Leo did find slightly odd, was the banner that curled beneath the wolves elegant paws. Where once a motto had been inscribed, there now sat a deep scar - someone had sabotaged the carving, but only decided to remove the words.

'Probably some dagger-happy soldier,' offered Alec, as if reading Leo's thoughts, tracing his fingers across the gauged out mark. 'Wreck, pillage, and plunder. Could have been any point in our history eh?'

'But why only remove the words?' said Leo.

'Maybe he took offence, or couldn't read.'

'Or it was written in a forbidden tongue,' said Isla with gravity.

Leo readied himself to ask what she meant, but Alec got in first, 'I wish your tongue was forbidden.'

'Thanks Al', love you too.'

Alec half-smiled and lowered his eyes, kicking nonchalantly at the ground. Mercia shot Isla a look, one eyebrow raised.

'Either way,' she said, 'it's pretty cool.' Scanning the other three, her eyes widened. 'Hey, guys.... where's Blake?'

'Over here!' came a shout from their left.

'What? Where are you?' said Mercia, confused, spinning on the spot; her dark hair billowing around after her.

'Not been kidnapped by a killer Otter too have you buddy?' called Alec.

Leo didn't like the tone Alec had just used. The sentence was fine, just the tone.

'You wha'?' came Blake's disembodied voice again. 'Seriously guys, you're all blind.'

By now they were all spinning on the spot, desperate to

prove him wrong, to find his hiding place.

'Look UP!' Blake chortled.

Leo stopped spinning, and let his eyes trace the crumbling wall in the direction of Blake's voice. There, in a crevice 12 foot off the ground, sat Blake recumbent and grinning.

'What the hell are you doing up there?!' cried Mercia.

'The King, when at the Castle, must at all times preside over his subjects, atop his throne,' and he mimicked a haughty gentleman, nose pointing skywards. 'Now, you there, boy -' he pointed to Leo, 'fetch me some courage so I can climb down.'

Leo stared back in sheer amazement. The man was insane. 'I can give you a hand?' Leo stuttered, 'But I'm afraid I don't have any courage to spare.'

'Haha, it's alright, everyone had enough here yeah?' said Blake as his hands changed positions on the rock as quick as the pictures in a flip book.

'Definitely,' said Alec coldly.

'Right then, as soon as I get down, we'll head off eh?' breathed Blake as his body contorted, his feet finding nothing but air and narrow perches.

'Be careful!' Mercia cried, her eyes fixed on him, her face blank and lips compressed.

'Yeah man, we don't want to be mopping up your blood,' said Alec and Mercia shot him a stern look. 'Well.. I don't anyway,' he mumbled and turned to face the direction of the car.

When Blake had reached a safe distance from the ground, about 4 feet up, he twisted so his back faced the wall, bent his legs slightly and jumped landing with a dull clomp. 'Right then,' he said as he stretched upwards, gritting his teeth. 'Let's go!'

'You idiot,' said Mercia as she hurried up beside him, retreating into his arm. 'Could've hurt yourself,'

'Ah well,' said Blake, shrugging.

Leo let the crowd file on before him, and felt the most peculiar sensation when he saw Isla and Alec fall beside each other, animatedly talking. He shook his head and ran his fingers through his hair. Just before the gap in the wall he took one last look around the Castle, determined to have it clear in his mind. Jacob would never believe this. This was better than anything he'd ever built in cardboard. The very stone itself seemed to shine with importance and dignity. He imagined how many floors there must have been, how many levels of wealth and what adventures they must have financed. Why had something this magnificent been abandoned? Or destroyed? He knew that war left nothing untouched, but there was usually a reason and he wished he could find out the reasoning behind this. Spinning on the spot he took one last look at the coat of arms and resolved to discover who they belonged to. It was then that something about the rest of the Castle caught his eye. Slightly above the large slab that was home to the heraldic banner lay three parallel marks in the rock.

He hadn't noticed them before, they were feint, not quite there - but standing at the gates, there they were, clear as day. As his eyes adjusted, they traced the rest of the remaining walls. They weren't the only ones. Here and there, scattered like acorns beneath an oak tree, those three parallel lines covered the walls of the castle. The angle and inclination changed, together with their length, but still they were there. Clearly some battle had taken place here; bayonets used perhaps. Though that didn't really make sense. As far as Leo knew, bayonets didn't have three points. Before he stepped beyond the threshold, he once again let his eyes fall upon the coat of arms, but this time at the banner which ran beneath the wolven feet. Sure enough, above and below the deep scar which had erased the motto that it had once bore, were two barely visible lines.

'Guys?' he said hesitantly. But there was no reply, the other three had walked too far to hear him. He'd mention it to them later. Anyway, it seemed they knew only about as much about the place as he did. With one last look back, he ran his hands through his hair, and broke into a jog to join the others. When he caught up with them the two pairs had merged once again and they were deep in conversation.

'---just sleep in the car,' Leo heard Alec say as he came beside them.

'No way,' said Isla, 'I'm not sleeping all hunched up. The tent won't take that long to set up.'

'Or we could stay at a hostel, they're pretty cheap, pretty comfortable,' said Mercia.

'Bit of a waste of money though eh?' Alec shot back.

'Well one night's not gonna break the bank is it? And by the time we get there we're not gonna want to set up a tent....' said Blake. 'Hey Leo, have you got any money on you?'

'Yeah,' Leo replied, 'but I don't know how much. What sort of prices are hostels?'

'About twenty quid? I'll pay for ya if you don't have enough- we're just thinking that we're gonna be driving for quite a while, and we'll probably need somewhere to crash as soon as we stop cause it'll be dark.'

Leo thought of the stack of notes he had hidden in one of the inner pockets of his backpack. He wasn't quite sure how much he'd taken that night, out of focus and determined, but he was sure that he could probably spend a good month in hostels on it.

'Yeah, that's no problem - I've got enough for that.'

'Excellent. Then it sounds like a plan.'

They reached the car and stopped, variously leaning on it or, in Alec's case, gently kicking the tyres. Blake fiddled with his pocket, trying to find his keys and Mercia checked her reflection in the wing-mirror. Watching the others, Leo felt a growing anticipation. Every journey they took led him further away from his life. He caught sight of his reflection in the car window and wondered, with a tinge of jealousy, how many of the people he was now standing with had welcomed in their adult age with the fundamental removal of their entire childhood. They'd all probably spent it with their loving, sober, truthful parents, siblings and strands of extended family. He imagined them one by one seated around a long table, fire glowing behind them and helium balloons, emblazoned with '18', tethered to the table and floating above them. He imagined them all being presented with a family heirloom, access to all the secrets of adulthood, and a toast being made in their honour - the finest champagne reaching the lips of their kin's shining faces and intensifying their warmth. Yet here he was, going down in flames; all that went before was now as distant and obscure as a dream. He was somebody else, and he did have a history. Everything has a history. Only this scholar didn't have the first idea where to look.

A cloud passed in the sky behind Leo, softening the sun's rays. His reflection became less distinct and his gaze passed through it. There, crumpled in the back seat lay a small brown envelope. His heart tightened and his pulse quickened.

'So where.... where are we going now?' he asked as Blake, who had now found the key, unlocked the car with a crunch.

'Fort Augustus,' replied Blake, flashing a grin at Leo, 'where else?'

The Imperial Court

The fire in the Office for the Minister of Intelligence crackled intensely. The coals shone a vibrant white and the remnants of wood from the last fire sent puce sparks flying onto the hearth. In the centre of this furnace twisted a long, iron pole. Surrounding the fire was a magnificent mantel of carved and polished marble. Above this hung an old oil painting, thick with black soot, depicting a great, muscular lion tearing into the neck of a fallen and skeletal unicorn. The light in the room was dim, coming only from the fire and one single floor lamp that leaned precariously against the wall in the corner of the room.

A knock sounded at the door and the Minister of Intelligence stopped turning the rod in by hand for a brief moment.

'Enter,' said the Minister of Intelligence loudly, voice carrying from the chair beside the fire to the entrance on the other side of the room. The Minister of Intelligence had been looking forward to this moment for quite some time. Nothing and no-one brought shame and failure to this House. Lessons had to be learnt.

The door opened and in stepped a dark-haired man, barely older than 25. His face had the pallor of a corpse and his movements were unsteady.

'You.... you asked to see me?' he said weakly.

'Take a seat,' said the Minister, gesturing to a hard wooden stool opposite the fire. The man did as he was told, rubbing his palms as he walked.

'Good,' continued the Minister, 'I asked to see you today to give you a chance to explain yourself.'

'Ex......ex....plain myself?'

'Oh come now Nickleson, you are aware, I am sure, what your gross irresponsibility and inadequate ability has cost us.' Nickleson took one glance at the rod the Minister was holding, revolving slowly within the flames and stoking the embers and immediately lowered his eyes to his knees.

'I did... everything I could....' he half whispered, 'it was out of my control. Everything went too fast... I-'

'You mean you had exactly what we wanted on a plate. All you had to do was deliver.' The Minister paused, and stared, quite hard into the depths of the furnace. 'One simple task. And yet..."everything went too fast"....' The Minister's gaze bore into Nickleson's eyelids. The fire cracked once more, and a flame licked the grate.

'You let us all down. Every.... single one of us.'

'I'm...s...s...ss...ss...'

'You're sorry, indeed. So, my dear, am I.' The Minister rose in the seat, back straight. 'Much as it pains me to do this. There must be repercussions for your actions. You must learn never to let us down again.'

Nickleson's eyes rose to meet the Minister's.

'Give me your arm.'

'Please... no.. I swear.... I did everything,' Nickleson sobbed.

'And now you'll do it better, won't you? Give me your arm.'

Nickleson raised his shaking arm, bit his tongue to try to make it hold steady and held it out, palm up towards the Minister, who grasped it, and pulled it closer to the chair.

'Please.... don't... do.... this.'

But the Minister's decision was already made. With one swift motion, she pulled the glowing iron rod from the coals and struck the soft pale flesh of Nickleson's right fore-arm.

'AHHHHHHHHHHHHHHHHHHHHHHHHHHHHHHHHH!!!!!'

The skin sizzled as it recoiled from the heat, burnt and dead, and a waft of smoke rose from the contact point. The Minister of Intelligence let the slightest hint of a smile cross her face as she smelt the peaty odour of burning flesh and heard his cries of exquisite pain. Crime had always deserved punishment, she thought. And failing to give your people what is expected of you is as odious a crime as any.

Casting the brand away she shook back her mane of ochre red hair and admired her handiwork. Where was once milken and supple, now lay the branded, deep red image of a lion passant, encircled by the words:

By Order of the I.C. - Failure I

Nickleson sat cradling his arm, the burning seeming only to have lessened, and not yet fully ceased. A single drop of dew fell from his eye and he stared into nothingness. The Minister eyed this creature with malleable disgust. She felt for him, he had been on such a pleasing path, had not failed her once. Once until she had really needed him. What a poor, pathetic waste. She sniffed the air, inhaled a pungent mixture of coal, wood-fire, and justice, and sank back in her seat, her skirt suit crumpling around her.

'How is our guest? Hmm?'

The figure before her grimaced; engulfed in pain, shaking violently from head to toe.

'I am asking you a question,' she hissed, 'Is your *one* redeeming factor settled in?'

'Yes.... yes..... she's across the hall,' he said through gritted teeth.

'Then what are we waiting for?' said the Minister, and rose elegantly from her seat. 'We must show our guests some manners.'

Her left eyebrow rose above her fringeline, and she walked towards the door to the Office, her high heels clipping along the wooden floor. Nickleson rose and, still clutching his arm, followed her out.

Stopping outside of the door that was immediately opposite her office, the Minister took a deep breath in, straightened herself up, and then pressed down on the cold brass handle to the Interrogation Room. 'This better not take all night' she thought to herself as she strode purposefully into the room leaving Nickleson to close the door behind her.

The Interrogation Room was a cavernous rectangle painted slate grey. In the four corners of the ceiling hung loudspeakers so old they looked as if they had been torn from gramophones. In the centre of the room stood a wooden table, seven feet in length, inclined at a 45-degree angle. Next to the wall stood a cabinet of open pigeon holes containing various papers. The Minister stopped briefly to browse the cabinet, running her index finger across the lines of separation and then, finding the correct hole - retrieved a stapled report and walked with it, around the table, her footsteps echoing in the spartan room. Watching her with admiration, Nickleson stood beside the lower end of the table, waiting for orders.

'So,' the Minister said icily, 'I will ask you this only once...' and her skin crawled as she looked over her papers to the table. There, secured by metal bonds, lay a woman dressed only in her underwear, her feet skywards and arms nearly to the floor. Her face was obscured by a layer of cloth, wrapped around her head.

'...where is he?'

'I... don't.. know,' sobbed the woman, gasping for breath, her voice like the beat of an insects wings.

'Wrong answer I'm afraid,' and the Minister gestured to Nickleson.

Stowed beneath the table was a metal watering can that sloshed and expanded as Nickleson grasped it with two hands and carried it over to the low end of the table. With a nod from the Minister, he started to pour the water directly over the lower half of the woman's face. The freezing liquid ran over her mouth and nostrils and she thrashed violently, her arms and legs twisting like a surfaced worm within the confines of her shackles. She made noises like a suffocating dolphin, gurgling as she gasped for air and her chest sounded like a sanding machine.

After less than twenty seconds, the Minister nodded again to Nickleson, who raised the can. The woman breathed deeply and loudly, coughing and spluttering. Resolute and blank-faced, the Minister spoke again.

'I will ask you again, creature, Where is he?'

'You.....' sobbed the woman, 'YOU TOOK HIM!!!!' she screamed and shook with desperate fury in her bounds.

'You pathetic excuse for an animal,' said the Minister, stepping closer to the table. 'Your choice is simple. Tell us now and be left in the comfort of a cage, or never leave this room.' She took the can from Nickleson, dismissing him to the side of the room.

'I will never tell you anything. Butchers, slaughterers, MURDERERS!!!' shouted the woman.

The Ministers eyes narrowed and her lips pursed. She lowered her head to the woman's ear and whispered: 'You foul abominations do not deserve to exist.' Immediately, she sprung back, tipped the can and unleashed the rest of the water.

Above the pitter-patter of drops descending onto the cold, hard floor, the screams of the woman could be heard throughout the building. When they reached the basement level, a man in a shadowy office smiled cautiously.

'Finally,' he breathed, 'some progress.'

*

The waters of the black loch gently stirred as the cautious wind lapped over them, three slithers of cloud were reflected on the surface rippling slowly as if the mountains on either side of the loch had left them petrified after ripping them apart. The waters absorbed all colours around them, transformed them into something more ethereal - like the ghost of a shade the pale aquas of the sky became murky ink-pot blues and the whites of the clouds turned grey, and tinged with the most delicate of pinks. The depths of the loch were impenetrable to light, and for centuries had guarded the place's most important secrets.

Beside the shore, three ripples spread out in succession and were finished with a low-key 'plip'. Blake had scoured the banks for the perfect pebbles, flat - with a slight point, and was now skimming them across the water.

'Come on Nessie!!' he shouted with enthusiasm. 'Here girl!'

Standing next to him, Leo admired the way Blake's stones never seemed to fail - the perfect spin causing three, four, five rings before finally giving way to gravity and the abyss below. He'd heard a lot of things about this loch, and had often dreamt of coming here, envisioned hours sat by the shore watching, hoping to catch a glimpse of what lay beneath. Now he was here, the myth and mystery of the place seemed to penetrate him like the deep bass of a treble amp and he felt increasingly uneasy about Blake's efforts to bait the famous beast.

'I've seen it on maps, and in pictures, but it's a lot bigger than I thought it would be,' said Mercia.

'Yeah,' agreed Leo, 'and a lot more beautiful.'

'Definitely, I mean just look at that reflection. I want to swim in it.'

'Go on then, I've heard Nessie likes human bait,' said Alec.

'It's pretty deep Merse, and something about it creeps me out,' said Isla.

'I still would.' She walked a little closer to the edge, 'But, maybe another day. I'm hungry now.'

'Aye, me too,' said Blake, using the last of his stones to coil a perfect six-bounce. 'Shall we go find a little pub or something?'

'I'm there already,' said Alec.

'Sure,' agreed Isla, and Blake turned to Leo, who was kicking at pebbles.

'You got enough money for this mate?'

Leo looked up, he'd been lost in thought, his imagination working overtime he'd considered the possibility of the pebbles being dinosaur eggs which hatched one by one and marched into the loch.

'Yeah, plenty,' he said, nodding at speed.

'Right then,' Blake addressed the group, 'Let's goooooooooooo.'

Truth was that Leo hadn't wanted to leave, he'd never felt less hungry in his life and the magnetism of the loch urged him to stay, to wait. Still, unwilling to part from the group, he followed them back through the field of sheep which they'd walked through to gain access to the water. He decided, as he dodged the manure on the field, jumping a stream which fed the loch, to order a drink and something small, something just enough to keep him going. As always, he was the last of the group, and Blake fell back to walk beside him.

'You ok man?' he asked, his eyes searching.

'Yeah... yeah I'm fine thanks - really enjoying the views.'

'Ok, you just seem a little lost that's all, I mean, I don't know how you are normally; maybe you are the quiet type, but I couldn't help thinking that things were getting to you?'

Leo thought getting to was an understatement. As hard as he'd tried to force things from his mind; his head kept spinning. Adopted. Lies. Kidnap. Letter. Jake.

'I'm just worried about my little brother really,' he replied, 'he's 16, still there, in that house.'

'What sort of kid is he? Cause, I mean, if he's anything like you and he's 16 - I'm sure he'd be more than able to look after himself.'

'No, it's not that,' he sighed, 'it's our parents, they.... well they're... difficult.'

'Difficult?'

'They, er… they.. drink. A lot. And when they do the tears in their relationship unstitch, and we... we get the fallout.'

'Ah... they're brilliant aren't they? Parents. I haven't seen my old man for two years.'

'Oh..'

'Aye, upped and left, ran off with some floozy. I found out that day. I had my most important swimming competition, was on track for gold. Obviously I was bloody nervous, and I kept searching for him in the crowd but he never turned up.'

'Blimey.'

'Seven years, he'd been at every practice, every race, every competition. And then one day he decided his family weren't good enough for him. He had a better offer than seeing his son accomplish something. And yeah...' he paused, his eyes scanning the backs of the three in front. 'Not a trace of him since.'

'Sorry to hear that mate.'

'Don't be. His loss. Haven't swum since though.'

'They really are idiots aren't they?'

'Aye. But unfortunately there's no course in parenting. When a bairn comes out of the hospital there's no teacher waiting by the doors saying: 'You watch what you do or you'll cause this kid some serious problems.' I personally think there should be. I know when I have kids I'm always gonna be there for 'em.'

'Definitely. And not take my problems out on them.'

'Aye.'

They crossed the road, lagging well behind the others, and saw them file into the doors of a tiny pub built entirely from the local sky-grey stone.

'I hope they do burgers. I'm really in the mood for a huge burger in a crusty roll,' said Blake, turning to Leo as he pushed open the thick wooden door to the pub. Maybe Leo would eat something after all.

*

A contented silence had fallen around the table in the corner of the Red Dragon. In front of every party were empty plates, the occasional chip or scraping of tomato sauce, all topped by scrunched serviettes - the near universal symbol for *'this is finished, please take it away.'* Leo and the others were all slumped in their seats. Some forward, resting on their elbows, toying with their drinks - others backwards, dangerously close to tipping their chairs. In the centre of the room stood the bar, where a man and a woman stood and chatted, next to them sat an American couple dressed head-to-toe in outdoors attire.

'Errrrrrrrrrrrr,' Mercia yawned, breaking the silence, 'excuse me.'

'Why? Where are you going?' asked Alec.

'Shut up blondey,' Mercia replied flatly.

'So what are we doing tomorrow then?' said Isla, ignoring them.

'I saw a signpost for cruises on the Loch, run every hour,' said Mercia.

'Nessie hunting! YES!' said Blake.

'Looks like it's settled then,' said Alec, and he looked at Leo, 'You comin'?'

''Course he is,' Blake cut in.

'Yeah,' nodded Leo.

'There we go!' Blake tapped the table with his fingers like they were drumsticks, his movements becoming faster and more energetic, his smile unceasing.

'Where does it go from Merse?' asked Isla.

'There's a little harbour-type thing, down by the bridge - you get it from there.'

'Well, everyone done? We should go check it out now, so we know the times and don't have to faff about in the morning,' said Blake, resting on the edge of his seat.

'Don't you think we should find somewhere to sleep first? I mean, there's bound to be a hostel around here somewhere but I think getting in is fairly important. I don't want to sleep in the car tonight hun,' said Mercia.

'Yeah, there is that, but then, where do we start looking?'

At that moment the bald barman, who had come to collect their plates, asked for the furthest plate away from him in the corner of the table and said: 'We have rooms available for hostel prices.'

Everyone looked up at him in disbelief, how did a place so small manage to fit in bedrooms to rent out? Carefully balancing the last plate on his pile he seemed to read the looks on their faces.

'They're in the building across the courtyard from us, twenty pounds a night. I can book you in if you're interested?'

'Oh!' said Isla.

'Yes please, if you could,' Blake replied, 'This is brilliant guys, a place to sleep right on our doorstep. All that's left to do now is play pool! Anyone in?'

'Aye, get your fifties out then,' said Alec and they both hopped up from the table.

'Drinks first man.'

'Right enough,' and they walked towards the bar.

Leo also stepped up from the table and asked 'Anyone know where the toilets are?'

'Through the door behind us and to the right,' said Mercia, 'We'll be in there,' she pointed to the long thin side room than ran next to the pub door and contained one pool table, a few chairs and various shelf perches for drinks.

'Cool, cheers.'

As he made his way to the door, Leo tripped slightly on the carpet that had bunched up before the doorway. He stumbled a bit, and rushed quickly into the toilet, feeling his cheeks fill with warmth. What an idiot he must've looked like. He caught himself in the mirror, his blonde hair positively glowing under the harsh halogen lighting. He thought he looked alright, a bit of a mess perhaps, a bit casual - but given the circumstances she couldn't expect anything else really. He touched the cut on his forehead, now hard and almost black from the healing process. Leo thought that if it was any bigger it would look like he had a bloody mammoth's tooth embedded in his skull, the platelets having pushed together like tectonic plates, raising a mountain of scab. How could she bare to look at this?

His lip, too, had split, and was velvet red. As his hand moved down from his head to his lip, to feel the contrast between smooth pink flesh and and hard red cut he saw it. His right wrist was scarlet with a rash that ran in a perfect ring around it.

'What the?' he said aloud, and looking down from the mirror, used his left hand to touch the rash. 'Ahhhhhhhhhh!' he half-shouted in pain. Whatever had caused him to black out the night he'd been kidnapped had more than left its mark and was clearly happy to dose him out fresh hurt. Instinctively he ran it under the cold tap, but this, if anything, only made it feel worse.

'Ow!! What the hell is this?' he shouted as he flinched from the water like an aquaphobic cat. Three times he turned his wrist over, slowly revolving it forwards and backwards, attempting to decipher what he'd worn or touched or eaten to cause a rash like that. He'd rolled out from a car, yeah, but it was mainly his shoulders and knees which paid for that. He'd ran through foliage, scratching every inch of him. But this was a perfect circle. He wasn't even tied up when he woke in the van, and the tell-tale signs of rope were missing.

Eventually, realising he hadn't done anything to warrant it, he sighed and pulled down his sleeve, holding it in place with the tips of his fingers. He'd keep an eye on it. If it got any worse he'd tell them, and ask to go to a Doctors'. He looked up at his reflection once more, ruffled his hair with his left hand and said 'Hey, maybe she likes the injured-veteran look.' It was a long shot, he knew, but he had to have hope.

When Leo found the others, they were involved in a heated game of doubles.

'TWO SHOTS!' shouted Alec as Mercia failed to make the white ball hit anything other than green velveteen.

'Oh shut up, I'll get you yet,' she said as she passed her

cue to Isla. 'Anyway, I don't really think this whole 'Boys v. Girls' thing is very fair...'

'Why? Because we're better than you?' said Alec as he lined himself for a promising shot on a red.

'No, because you've spent far too much time in pubs endlessly shooting at random. And now your random shots have morphed into the jammy kind.'

'What? Babe that makes no sense,' laughed Blake.

'I knew what she meant,' said Isla, 'and whilst I'd disagree with her thinking we couldn't beat you, you are clearly more practised than us.'

'You can say that again,' said Alec as he comfortably potted two balls in succession.

Mercia stared blankly at him. 'Well next time,' she said, 'I propose mixing the teams.'

'And that's....,' called Alec as the black ambled calmly towards its exit, falling with a satisfying *clunk* 'GAME!'

'You may have won the battle, but we'll win the war.' said Isla.

'I'm shaking,' mocked Alec and Blake chuckled.

'Arrrrghhhhhhh!! You--'

'Anyway, good game, but Leo's back,' said Blake.

'Ah yeah, right, Leo,' said Isla as they all looked at him. 'We've decided, that if you want to go to that address tonight, before it gets too late - I can take you.'

'You can...,' started Leo.

'I'm lending her the car,' Blake explained.

'Ohhh.'

'Yeah, so, I mean if you want to, now that we're all settled in for the night. Entirely up to you though. These guys will stay here and no doubt drink themselves into a stupor.'

'Oi!' said Alec.

'Like it's not true,' and she rolled her eyes.

'Fair point,' he conceded, raising his pint glass to his mouth.

'What do you think?' She held Leo's gaze.

Leo wished the eagles would disappear from his stomach again, he was tired of being an impromptu aviary, but her stare had him lost and he couldn't move.

'I....I...' he stammered, coughed and then regained himself. 'Yeah, that would be great,' he lied. As much as he wanted to be alone with Isla again, his stomach sank at the thought of going to that orphanage. After that there would be no turning back. Unless of course he hit his head hard against the wall and forgot everything. But he knew, if he did do that, he'd be in an even worse position than he was now. Atleast now he had some history, even if its pretext was false.

'Excellent,' chirped Isla and her face lit up, 'shall we go to the car?'

'Iz, have you got your phone yeah?' said Alec as she put down her cola and walked towards Leo.

'Yes, Dad,' she giggled, 'Yeah,' and she pulled her mobile out of her jeans pocket, 'right here.'

'Good, we'll be here when you get back ok?'

'Al..... right,' and she screwed her face up and cocked her head to the side. 'Let's go,' she murmured to Leo, pushing him towards the door.

'See you guys later!' called Blake. 'Drive carefully.'

'Will do.'

And they walked out of the pool room and opened the pub door.

'IZ!' shouted Mercia.

'What now?' said Isla quietly to Leo, 'YEAH?' she called back.

'Text me!'

Isla smiled, 'O.K!....Right, let's go!'

They walked out of the pub and into the cool night air, the stars above them shining in earnest while there were no clouds to smother their light. The Moon rose in the east and Isla's hair was the sun lighting Leo's path. When they reached the long stretch of path, from where they could see the car, all the bustle of town had dissipated and they were alone, their every sound - footsteps, heartbeats, magnified tenfold within the shadow.

'So,' said Isla, pushing her hair behind her ear, 'are you excited?'

'More nervous to be honest. Like, I'm not sure how I feel. How I should feel,' he paused.

'I mean, don't get me wrong, I want to know and everything. It's just abit... weird. Everything's happened so quickly. Three days ago I'd never been to Scotland, yet here I am. I didn't know I was adopted and yet here I am with the address of the orphanage I was put into... It's all.... '

'No, it's okay, I understand. You don't have to talk about it, and if you want - when we get there I can just sit in the car and wait?'

'No, no,' Leo fought hard to keep the anvil from crushing his chest, 'I'd like you to be there, if ....?'

'Yeah, I'll come with,' she smiled at him, outshining all the stars.

They reached the car, hopped in and Isla turned the key in the ignition, firing up the heating.

'I warn you now,' she said as she rubbed her hands together, 'I'm not the best of drivers.'

'At least you can drive. I've failed a couple of tests.'

'Ahh, well to be fair I don't know how I managed to pass mine. I reckon the examiner was having a good day. I'm convinced I almost ran over an old woman and he didn't notice.'

'What? Like forgot to stop?' Leo said, scrunching his eyes up.

'No, I couldn't see her, she was so small. It was only when I heard the bump of the zimmer-frame I knew I was in trouble.' They both collapsed with laughter.

'Haha.... yeah... so like I say, my driving is terrible and if we die, I'm sorry.'

'Nah, I'm sure we won't. I have faith in you. Granny-killer.'

'Oi!'

'So, do you know where we're going?'

'No, but I've got the handy Sat-Nav,' she said, waving at the small black box plugged to the centre of the dashboard. 'Have ye got the address?'

'Yeah,' and he reached into the back seat of the car and took the letter from his bag, 'it's: Aloysius Building, Pére David's Orphanage, Fort Augustus, PH32 7NU.'

'Got it, just waiting for it to load.....' and she rubbed the inside of her legs with her palms, 'There we go! Right, seatbelts on? Let's go!' She released the handbrake and they began to move.

'Is it far away?'

'Only about ten miles, apparently.'
'Ten miles!?'
'Haha, it'll only take us about ten minutes, stop worrying.'
'Well, I just hate being a nuisance.'
'You aren't a nuisance at all, I for one am glad you're here actually. A refreshing change from my lot. Don't get me wrong, I love them all. But after 6 weeks on the road, anyone can get a bit much,' she waved her free hand towards the glove box, 'Fancy putting on some music?'

'Sure,' said Leo as he leant down to open the compartment, but as hard as he tried, it wouldn't budge. The mechanism was stuck somehow.

'You have to squeeze!' laughed Isla.

'Oh... right... that might be why.' He squeezed either side of the keyhole and the compartment released itself. Inside sat a map, an electronic charger Leo assumed was for the Sat-Nav and an mp3 player. A wire from the mp3 player dangled and disappeared into the belly of the car.

'Any requests?' he said as he began to scour the extensive collection.

'Nope, whatever you like. I'm quite interested to hear your taste in music.'

Leo found his favourite band and the perfect song and with a tap the guitar and bass were playing a harmonic, synthesised intro. Anthemic and inciting.

'Good choice!' shouted Isla above the falsetto shrieks of the lead singer. 'Are you a bit of an indie fan?'

'Yeah, I guess so,' Leo had never really considered this before. He just liked anything with a good beat, energy and insightful lyrics, 'but I'm into anything really.'

'Me too, I honestly believe that if you're a music purist, you're not a true fan.'

'Absolutely,'

The road stretched ahead of them, surrounded on either side by high trees and hedgerows, twisting and turning like the trail of pouring glue. Sitting here beside her, Leo felt freer and more pristinely alive than he'd ever done before.

'So, what made you come on the trip?' he asked.

'What? This, as in to the orph -?'

'No, no, the road-trip.'

'Oh, well, basically thanks to my parents, I've holidayed all around the world you know - flown to New York, Spain, Portugal, Morocco, Eurostar for weekends in Paris. But I'd never been around Scotland. My own country. And I realised that seeing as we have some of the most powerfully beautiful landscapes in the world, for me to keep seeing those other places without visiting here would be entirely perverse. Not to mention all the damage flying causes. I've resolved that when I travel elsewhere it will always be with emissions in mind. Trains are supposed to be pretty good.'

Leo looked at her with an expression akin to perplexion, but in truth was respect of the highest order.

'Yeah... I know,' she said, raising her eyebrows, 'I'm abit of a hippy I suppose. The environment's kinda my thing........... she says as she drives a fossil fuelled pollution machine around the wilderness.' and laughed.

'If I'm honest I can't think of a better interest.'

'You don't have to say that you know. I'm used to people calling me a flower-child.'

'No, I honestly believe it.'

She turned to look at him, head on its side, 'O.K.'

'So, have you ever done anything direct? Like a.... ' Leo struggled to think of terminology, 'A sit-in or protest or anything?'

'Not had the chance to go to any yet. There's a big one coming up later this year protesting against new coal-fired stations which I'll definitely be going to. But a few years ago, 'cause I live on the coast, there was this big oil slick from a tanker that covered seabirds and otters and things - I spent three days on the beach, cleaning. First the animals, then the beach. I've not felt right about driving since. I can't tell you the amount of times I threw up.'

'Wow, that's really cool.'

'What, throwing up?' said Isla sarcastically.

'Haha, no, no the cleaning. You-,' he caught himself, '.. it's pretty amazing.'

'I wish I didn't have to do it to be honest. But it's a natural reaction, I guess I have some sort of affinity with animals. They never make you promises they can't keep.' She paused briefly, indicating for a left turning. 'Before my Mam and Dad split up, our house was full of animals. You name a pet, we had it. And more.'

'Cool.'

'Anyway you, come on, tell me about your interests. What do you like?'

'Reading, films... mainly art-house or foreign, camping, hiking.'

'And I bet you're lucky enough to have friends who're into the same things aren't you?'

'No, actually. I mean, yeah, I have 'friends' or people I can go places with, talk to. But as far as my interests go, I have to entertain them alone. I suppose I've never had a 'best friend' figure, just fleeting groups of them.' Leo had never said any of this to anyone before. The more he spoke, infact, the more he was shocking himself. Psycho-analysis via attraction. Interesting.

'Well, I think I can safely say - you can say hello to your first non-temporary friend. Or rather, group of them. The others really like you too.'

Now this Leo didn't believe. There wasn't a chance that Alec liked him. 'Are you sure?'

'Yeah, Blake was raving about you earlier. How nice you are.'

'Oh... I don't think Alec likes me very much though.'

'What makes you say that?'

'I don't know, just the way he is to me.'

'Don't worry about him, he's like that with his mother. And he loves her to bits.'

'Oh yeah by the way, are you two....?'

'Eh?'

'Are you two, you know, together?'

Isla flung her head round in shock, her mouth gaping open. 'Wha....? No.. Never!'

CRUNCH

Isla and Leo were flung violently forward in their seats, the car began to skid. Isla quickly grabbed the steering wheel and turned into the spin.

'WHAT THE HELL WAS THAT!?'

'I...... I don't..... know,' replied Leo breathlessly as the car rolled to a halt. It couldn't be them. Not again. How would they know where he was? His heartbeat rose faster and faster, both of them were breathing sharply - gasping for air like a surfaced diver.

'Blake's gonna kill me!' shouted Isla as her face drained of all colour.

'Well... well.... let's find out what it was first before we make assumptions. The car could be okay for all we know,' said Leo, though he had no desire to leave the relative safety of the glorified tin-can they were in. It was dark, and they were in the middle of nowhere.

'Whatever we just hit had to have been pretty big to knock us off course like that.'

'God, I hope it wasn't a person....'

'SHHHHHHHHHHHHHHH! No, no, it wasn't, it definitely wasn't, it can't have been.'

'There's only one way to be sure.' Leo sounded far more certain than he felt.

'Aye. Count of three? One.'

'Two....'

'Three,' they said simultaneously, each pulling the door lever as fast as they could.

As Leo rounded the front of the car to be at Isla's side, the fog which had descended over his panic-stricken mind began to lift and he became very aware that regardless of what they hit, they would not be able to remain where they were for any length of time. The car had, though expertly handled by Isla, spun almost a full 90 degrees and stretched across the road causing a would-be blockage to any approaching vehicle. To make matters worse, this particular stretch of road had no form of street lighting. The trees that engulfed either side of it seemed to whisper with the voices of ghosts.

Illuminated to a perfect jaundice by the miserable warmth of the headlights, stood Isla, her back facing Leo. Under such a lamp her treacle hair was burnt to a crisp black, its tips like strings of caramel rose and fell with the gentle breath of the wind. Leo walked towards her, his body breaking the beam and caught sight of the car's bumper. A large dent in the centre was accompanied by flecks of missing paintwork and the registration plate was at an obscure position.

'Woah...' he said, 'Well, it's not too bad.... fixable at least....'

'Oh, Leo,' said Isla without turning to him. Something about her tone wasn't right. He walked over to her and saw two solitary tears streak down her face.

'Hey! What's up? C'mon you...' his insides twisted.

'Look,' She raised her hand, indicating a spot on the road not 8 feet from them. There, splayed across the centre of the road lay a magnificent Red Stag. A pool of black was spreading slowly from it, gorging on the yellow tarmac. Leo felt his throat tighten. He'd heard stories of people hitting deer on the roads up here, but never in a million years thought it would happen to him. He rested his hand on Isla's welcoming shoulder, whose own rose to meet his.

It was then that it happened. A feeling inside him began to bubble, and a sensation much like hunger overcame him. His eyes narrowed, and he focussed intently on the fallen stag. Without a word to Isla, he began to walk towards it. He had no idea what he was doing, but with every step the sensation became stronger. His arm stretched behind him as Isla refused to let go.

'Leo! What are you doing!? It's dead!' but he didn't reply and his hand tore from her grip. 'Leo!!' her voice became distant, insignificant, one of a thousand that he heard from every direction. When he came to the beast he sank to his knees, wetting them with blood. The stag was on its side, its legs facing the way they'd came and across its upper flank, from its neck to its foreleg, stretched a laceration caused by the impact. The shades of graduated grey to black showed Leo where the blood had matted the fur.

Still, slowly, but with some regularity, its chest rose and fell. Waves of neuro-messages crashed over Leo like a tempest and his blood was sherbet powder. With one hand, he grasped an antler and clenched tight, with the other he pressed his open palm with full force into the gaping wound. His eyes seared and the tingling through his body gave way to shattering pain.

'AHHHHHHHHHHHH!' He tried to pull away, but it was no use, his hands were fused to the flesh and bone of the stag. Spluttering, he gasped for air as all his muscles contracted and his nerves burned. The Nausea within him rose like a helium balloon and his diaphragm vibrated incessantly. Two single tears wound their way down his cheeks and with one last great pull - he released his hands, slumped over onto them, and threw up.

'Are you ok!!?' shouted Isla as she ran over to Leo, but did not get further than half way. The sight of the impossible stopped her in her tracks.

The stag raised its head, dumbly at first, and then with intent, and as it did, it threw itself into a lying position. The wounds it had were closed, smooth skin replacing bloodied flesh. Its powerful neck turned slowly through a full 180 degrees, it opened its mouth wide and twisted its ears. Tentatively, as though it were an old man lifting himself from a low chair, it began to shuffle from side to side, and then slip one leg out at a time, hauling itself up. When it stood in full stride, antlers included, it was far taller than Isla, and the equal of Leo who was now spitting and shaking in shock - his white eyes wide in disbelief and terror.

Some minutes passed with the three figures rooted to their individual spots on the road, none making a sound or daring to move. The ennui was broken only when the stag lowered its enormous weapons in Leo's direction and bolted for forest, absorbed once again by the endless night from whence it came.

'What.... what did you just do?' Isla stammered. 'That stag was de- and then you... you touched it and...' Leo's insides were churning. She was right. He had just done something. Something he couldn't explain. Something he couldn't help. He'd acted solely on impulse and ended up vomiting.

'I really don't know,' he said, and wiped his mouth with his arm.

'And what the hell is wrong with your wrist!!!?' she shouted.

Where the rash had been easily concealable though horrifically red and blotchy, his skin where the rash had been was now blistered, the flesh scored in raised pockets shaping characters than ran around the ring.

'What?' Leo sheepishly tried to hide it, 'Oh, nothing; caught it I suppose.' He winced as his sleeve drew over it, 'Atleast... atleast the deer was alright in the end.' Leo concluded that whatever kind of lunacy had overtaken him in the last few minutes and led him to sit in a pool of blood was not going to win the battle. The animal had been in shock. Nothing more.

'But it was pouring with blood before you -'

'Just a little scratch. Have you never had a tiny cut that's seeped with the stuff?' He hauled himself up onto his feet. In the cold yellow light it looked as though he'd been playing in tar. His hands and jeans were oozing black. Isla stared at him, mouth hanging slightly open.

'Seriously, little scratch,' and he wiped his hands onto the top half of his jeans to clean them. 'Shall we go?'

'Wha..... You can't be serious.... the car!?'

'The car's fine, there's only a tiny bump.'

'And your jeans....?'

'That'll dry soon, and I'm not gonna be touching anything in the front seat am I?'

Isla's hair blew in the wind and she eyed him much as one would look at a person trying to open a door with their bare feet on Clapham High Street. She then shook her head.

'I... really don't understand you Leo.. whateveryourlastnameis.'

'Hall.'

'Leo Hall..... I like it.'

'Yeah, I did too.'

'Anyway. Leo Hall. You confuse and astound me.'

'Are we going then?'

'Well considering you're going to force your abattoir attire in Blake's car regardless of what I say; it certainly looks that way.'

'Brilliant,' said Leo and walked back to the car.

Mr. Elbridge's Secret

For the rest of the journey, neither party spoke, which was fine by Leo. He was trying to get his head straight. What had actually happened after he'd left Isla's side back there? He knew he'd never felt like that ever before. Passion, yes. Empathy, yes - but never pure, instinctual magnetic attraction. What was the deal with his wrist? It was throbbing. He'd never fantasised so much about painkillers before in his life. He felt like all his energy was drained and was dreading, more than ever, having to find out about the past he never knew in this pathetic state. He knew he'd probably be sat in the hygiene-white office of some smarmy, happy-go-lucky chap - biting his lip to stop himself from screaming in agony. Still. One part of him wanted answers.

As the sat-nav directed them left into the final road, a solitary sign stood sentinel before the long dark approach.
               Pére David's Orphanage
               Comprising: Aloysius
               Buildings   Christopher
                            Andrew
               PLEASE DRIVE SLOWLY.
               VISITORS PLEASE REPORT TO ALOYSIUS Room A2

'It looks like the one we want is the first one we come to,' said Isla, dropping down a gear.

'Where the bloody hell is it?' asked Leo after they'd driven for 5 minutes in the suffocating darkness of the approach road.

'It's gotta be, hang on...' Isla pushed her face closer to the windscreen. The headlights before them were beginning to create shadows out of something a few feet before them, '...what's that?' She slowed the car down and the wheels began to make a welcome crunch on the beginnings of a pebbled drive. There, before them, erupting from the ground like a bleak mid-winter oak were giant, wrought-iron gates painted black.

The letters PERE DAVID'S ORPHANAGE ran across the top curve of the gate, shadowed by enormous spikes shooting into the air. On either side of the opening lay a lion, their mouths supporting the locking mechanism. Both the letters and lions were finished in gold-leaf, which glinted under the car lights. Beyond the gates stretched the remainder of the pebble driveway, carpeting the floor surface before and around three disjointed and imposing buildings made of deep tea-spoon grey stone. Between each building ran a sheltered walkway, their pillars in the same wrought iron as the gate, connecting their three great hulks into a cohesive whole.

'I think we might just have found it,' said Leo, feeling cold.

'It looks like a cross between a prison and a stately home,' said Isla, her finger playing despondently with a gold keyring hanging from the ignition.

'Yeah.... not exactly how I'd imagined an orphanage to look to be honest.'

'Have you never seen Oliver Twist?'

'Good point. But, this is the 21st century - not the 19th.'

'They're not just going to knock it all down are they?' She paused, drinking in the misery of the scene, 'Creepy as it is.' She turned the key in the ignition, shutting off the engine. The interior light to the car came on.

'Right...ready?'

'Yeah,' Leo lied. In truth he wanted to be as far away as possible from this place. He wanted to see Jacob, to lie in his bed and read, not be in the middle of nowhere, having been an accomplice to a hit-and-stun and covered in animal blood for the second time in as many days. Still, she was here - not there.

They got out of the car, and whilst Isla locked it, Leo walked closer to the gates, searching for any hint of familiarity. The only thing that offered any subconscious trigger was the two lions. He'd seen far too many coins in his years at the shop. He'd once asked his Dad why there was a lion on the back of the ten pence piece and a rose on back of the twenty, but was told to 'quit playing with it and stick it in the till, boy'. It was later that day he'd been given his first proper pay-packet. 'There'll be plenty of little Leos in there for you to look at,' his Dad had winked at him, with a pat on the back.

Grasping the ice-cold railing, a careful smile sprang to Leo's lips. He found it funny the things he could remember so vividly, instances so seemingly non-formative - yet ask him to recount his eighth birthday party and he'd be at a loss; reaching for falling confetti in the pouring rain.

'How do you think we get in?' asked Isla, who was now beside him and turning her head this way and that.

'Err...' That was something Leo hadn't considered. It was real. That was enough for him. Following directions from a letter written by a stalker 'saint' was sheer madness. For them to actually lead somewhere was a fair degree beyond crazy. But then, given that someone clearly wanted him dead and he'd just forced his hand into the gaping flesh of a deer, that level seemed like it was becoming the norm, ' ..there's no lights on, maybe there's nobod-'

'Found it,' interrupted Isla, who'd moved to the gate's edge, nestled in beside the hedgerow.

'Found... what?' Leo's eyes widened.

The buzzer,' she nodded her head to the height of her hips, where, sure enough a small box was attached on to the railings. 'We call, they ask who we are, we go in.'

'But-'

It was too late, Isla's finger had already forced down hard on the little red button. For ten seconds they waited, for nothing.

'Told you, they're not at-' but a low hum then began to emit from the box, followed by a crackling. A strained voice came over the speaker.

'Who.... who is it?' rasped a light voice of a man.

Leo and Isla looked at each other for a second, eyebrows raised.

'Oh, hello, sorry to disturb you,' Isla said, bending down to the box, 'I wonder if you could help us. I'm here with my friend who's just found out he's a former,' she paused, searching desperately for the right word, '...resident... of yours and would like to know a bit more about.... well... himself.'

'Come, come.... Room A2, first building on the left,' said the man and there was a clicking in the background.

Suddenly, the jaws of the golden lions began to widen as if they were letting out a silent roar and a mechanism clunked with the chink of metal-on-metal to unbar the gate latch. Steadily, they swung inwards, scraping the pebbles like a priceless watch upon a redbrick wall.

With a sideways glance at one another, both Leo and Isla crossed the threshold to the Orphanage and headed for the first building on the left.

'Are those actual gas lamps?' asked Isla, indicating two old-fashioned black-paned lamps hanging from posts at either end of the gate.

'Looks like it.'

'Okay, I'm now officially expecting to see a rotund governor and a haggard old washerwoman.'

'Just don't ask for more,' he grinned.

'Why couldn't you have had some nice homely orphanage,' she shivered.

'Think about those words. Nice,' he paused for effect, 'Homely - great. Orphanage - not so much.'

'Well, your parents were either rich or powerful for you to end...' she trailed off.

'What?'

'Sorry, I've just realised... I'm being completely insensitive.'

'No, it's fine, I like it, it's cool.'

She raised an eyebrow. 'You like me being insensitive?'

'Haha, well, no - but I like the way you are.' Leo wondered if those words actually left his lips. 'What I mean is... I can tell by your tone you're jovial.'

'Ahh... that's cool then. I forget that I've only just met you, I'm used to the banter between Alec and Blake on the road.'

'Don't worry about it, you're only saying what I'm thinking,' he paused 'Mostly.'

They approached the end of Aloysius building, finding enormous wooden double-doors blocking their path. Leo rushed to open one, to let Isla in. But as she passed, she stopped and turned to him.

'Now, just.... don't go bursting into song on me okay? I sound like a seagull choking on a particularly rotten oyster.'

Leo's cheeks hurt. He really was so glad she'd made him come.

The wooden doors lead to a long corridor, originally painted what appeared to be sky blue but mould and neglect had long-since taken their toll. Chips had flaked from the paintwork and where once the handpainted clouds at the tops of the walls had been white and fluffy they were now ashen, making the corridor appear less like a calm summer's day and more the aftermath of a hurricane. Pressed up against the wall halfway down the corridor was a battered wooden chair of the sort you'd find in a second-rate antiques warehouse. On it sat the sole apparent survivor of the storm. Threadbare in places due to years of loving abuse, a sandy-brown teddy bear sat sentinel and stoic, its expression bemused but its arms welcomingly forward and urgently calling for a cuddle.

'Maybe they weren't rich,' Isla stated, matter-of-factly, as their footsteps ricocheted from hard stone tile to bare dank wall.

'I doubt it's always been like this,' said Leo.

'Well it looks like no one's done any work on the place for a while.'

'Do you think it's still open?'

'It must be, otherwise why would there still be someone working here?' She ran her palm along the wall and then inspected it, her face screwed up, 'Though quite what work they're doing is beyond me.' They reached the end of the passage and in front of them snaked off two further corridors, one hard to the left, the other hard to the right. 'What room did he say again?'

'A2.' In truth, Leo hadn't the faintest idea which room the man had told them to go to, but seared into his memory was the combination from the letter.

'Well there's A1,' said Isla, and pointed down the corridor to their right. Leo's eyes fell on a large silver plaque mounted beneath a maths-paper window in the centre of the first door on their right. 'It'll be further down, come on.'

When they finally reached room A2, which was a fair distance past A1, they noticed immediately the lack of window in the door, and the identifying plaque seemed to be larger - as if to compensate. Beneath the room number, in a bold and proper script, was engraved the name:

D. Elbridge

After both stopping to take a breath, the pair exchanged a silent look and, nodding to Isla, Leo tapped gently on the door.
    'Enter.....' growled a voice from inside, and Isla took the handle.
    As the door yielded to her push, a spacious and Spartan office was revealed. The lights that were embedded in the ceiling illuminated the room with a mock-daylight, cold and harsh. The change from dilapidated, whimsical corridor to this space could not have been more pronounced. Where before the walls, though damp and peeling, had shone with the remnants of colour and joy - here every surface was gleaming white and the air was entrenched with the sickening smell of lemon. Clustered together in sporadic groups along the sides of the walls were filing cabinets of uniform size, shape and material. Their shining steel surfaces reflected the light from above and they became mirrors, the room growing in their stead. At the far end of the room just in front of a great window sat their host on a wide desk of white laminate.
    Dressed immaculately in a white shirt and slate trousers, the man was fiddling with papers spread out before him on the desk as Leo and Isla approached. Looking up briefly, he pushed his thick-rimmed glasses back onto the bridge of his nose.
    'Do have a seat,' he said, and they both obeyed, taking their place like so many other desperate cases in front of the desk. 'Now,' and he skilfully tidied his papers into two separate piles in front of him, 'what can I do for you?'
    'Well.. I...' began Leo, but his tongue failed him. The business-like manner in which the man was dealing with them had left him completely disarmed. He hadn't come to order a new sofa, make a complaint or ask for a repeat prescription. He was here to shed some light on a particularly painful piece of news.

'As I said at the gate, my friend has very recently found out that he was adopted as a child,' her eyes flicked between Leo and the man, 'and has been informed, rightly or wrongly, that he was in care of this orphanage for the first part of his life.'

'Mmmhmm,' acknowledged the man, now staring at Leo's blood-soaked jeans.

'We were wondering, if perhaps..... whether you have any information you'd be able to give us on the circumstances of him coming here? Or of his time here? I'm sure you appreciate it would mean a great deal.'

'Well now,' said the man, his eyes piercing into Leo's, 'that might be something I can help you with. What did you say your name was, son?'

'Leo. Leo Hall, and that's Isla.'

'Right,' he replied, his eyes widening slightly 'if you two would just give me a moment, I can check our records for you. Don't have to go far,' he smiled and nodded towards the filing cabinets behind them.

'Yes, yeah, brilliant, thanks,' said Leo. The man got up, and his silvering hair rippled the light like the scales of a freshly caught fish. Leo's gaze traced downwards and caught a glint of gold from a chain hanging at the man's neck. When the man moved off behind them, he dropped his eyes and they fell on the desk where Leo noticed, for the first time, a sign, written in the same font as the plaque on the door:

Mr. Daniel Elbridge
CHIEF GOVERNOR

'What's your date of birth?' called Mr. Elbridge from behind them. Leo strained round to see him leaning over one half-opened drawer of the closest cabinet.

'The first of August, 1989.'

Mr. Elbridge closed the drawer and moved three cabinets down to resume his search.

When Leo turned his head back round, his eyes focussed on the wall beside Isla. From ceiling to floor it was covered in clip-framed photographs of smiling children and babes in the arms of their new parents. Leo wondered whether his had called the police yet, whether, even, they'd snapped out of their own self-obsession and realised he'd gone. He raised his hand to his mouth to chew his fingernails, but as he did so his blistered wrist caught on the inside of his sleeve and he let out a yelp of pain. Both Isla and Mr. Elbridge looked at him.

'Everything alright?' said Mr. Elbridge from a crouching position, his arms in the lowest of one of the drawers.

'Yes.. fine... thanks,' said Leo through his teeth, clutching his arm and he looked at Isla, whose smooth face was blank; both sides of her hair tucked behind her ears. A slam of the drawer behind them shook them from their thoughts.

'Are you absolutely sure it was this orphanage you were taken to?' said Mr. Elbridge, returning to the desk.

'Well, no, but I was...' said Leo, then thought it wouldn't be such a good idea to tell the governor of an orphanage the exact circumstances of how he came to know where he'd been adopted from '...told that this was the one.'

'Right.... right.' said Mr. Elbridge and he moved back around the desk to take his seat. 'The reason I ask is because, I am afraid, there are no records whatsoever of a child of your name or date of birth ever spending time at this institution. It seems that whoever told you that you were here was mistaken.'

'Oh...' Leo felt the stone inside of him sink even deeper. He couldn't breathe.

'I am really very sorry, but there is not much else I can do. However..,' and he squared the sides of the two piles in front of him 'whereabouts do you live?'

'Hertfordshire, England,' responded Leo, and Elbridge's face twisted. '...but I'm staying in Fort Augustus at the moment, though I don't know how long for. Why's that?'

'Because there are resources available at local libraries - lists of the orphanages in the area, and indeed, Scotland-wide. Chances are that whoever it was that told you may have gotten this mixed up with the correct one. A few phone calls and you should find it eventually.'

Leo fell silent and his eyes dropped to the floor. The shred of hope he'd had had stretched beyond its limit and splintered and shattered. The pain in his wrist became more intense and he bit down hard on his tongue.

'You're certain there was no record?' said Isla.

'Absolutely... I've been Governor here for 25 years and the records we keep are painstaking. We appreciate there are always going to be situations such as this.'

'Yeah.'

'I'm sorry I couldn't be more help. I'll see that the gates are open for you.'

'Thanks,' said Isla, and she rose from her seat.

'Yeah, thanks,' mumbled Leo as he did the same. The last thing he wanted to do now was speak.

'Safe journey,' said Mr. Elbridge as they opened the door to leave.

'Thank you,' replied Isla, and she pulled it shut with a subtle thud.

The silence of the corridor was palpable. Leo was on autopilot, staring at the floor and forcing himself to breathe.

'Well.... ' said Isla as they rounded the corner to the entrance hall, '...he was strange. Did you feel like you were applying for a bank loan too?'

'Yeah.'

'Oh Leo, don't worry. Like the guy said, there's lists available in libraries. We'll find out in the end.'

'Yeah,' he couldn't look at her.

'Come on,' she took his hand, 'let's get back to the others, with any luck they won't be drunk and we can get you a couple in.' she squeezed his hand and the nausea began to lift. 'Seconds thoughts...,' she added, '...here's hoping they're all abit too drunk to notice that bump in the car.'

They reached the entrance to the Aloysius building and stepped out into the cold night air, their footsteps crunching once more on the pebbled driveway. The moon had debuted in the sky and cast her radiant shimmer upon them.

It would be less than two nights before it was full once again.

'Hello......... Yes......... Hello Minister.' Daniel Elbridge spoke quickly into his mobile phone. 'Yes, indeed, just as you said.' His free hand traced inside his shirt collar. 'He has company.'

He pulled on the golden chain around his neck, releasing the pendant to the air.

'No, normal. Young and Scottish.' He raised the pendant slowly to his eye level and twisted it this way and that.

'Everything you asked. He's none the wiser.' He smiled. Reflected in his pupils was the shape of the pendant. A tiny, golden lion that he turned between his fingers.

'Yes. By the way, thanks to your organisation for the recent generous donation.' His smile widened and he placed the lion between his teeth for a second.

'And Minister?.... When will I see you?' He let the lion fall to his shirt and fumbled in his trouser pocket.

'Done. Goodbye.' He ended the call and placed the phone down on the desk. From his pocket he produced a cigarette lighter. Picking up the pile of papers to the left, he held them by the top corner, flicked the lighter and held it beneath. The flames caught the pile, the top of which was a form, old and well handled. He threw the pile into a wire mesh bin on the floor beside him and flames engulfed it within seconds. The paper turned brown, blackened to ask and then fell to the bottom. The last intelligible line of the form was an inch from the top:

Mother's Name: Rhoswen

Standing to be away from the acrid smoke, Daniel picked up the last pile of papers from his desk and paced towards the door. Time was of the essence. Now that they were sure, the Passanters would need every scrap of information they could get.

The Black Loch

'The Loch, in fact, all three of the great Lochs that run almost diagonally through the Highlands sit on a massive fault-line in the Earth's crust. On the one side, the mountains are, geologically speaking, very young. On the other, they're incredibly old. This fault-line is one of the many reasons why these Lochs are so deep. In fact, this Loch at its deepest point is almost 745 feet deep,' said John, the guide, leaning up against the side of the cruise boat.

The group had decided that morning that Nessie-hunting would be the day's agenda. Cruising down a peaceful Loch with enough fresh air to wake the dead was just what the doctor ordered after a night of mayhem. That and they didn't have to move.

Sadly, though, the friendly old tour-guide was bearing the brunt of their pallid faces and panda eyes. Accustomed to the searching questions of eager Americans or the rapid-flashing of Japanese cameras, the doe-eyed group of youngsters found him working harder than ever to fill the blank spaces. He'd told them of the flora and fauna that lived in the Loch, why in fact they were 'Lochs' and not 'Lakes' ('Because they're Scottish') and other tidbits included in his well-planned itinerary. But his company hadn't provided for, nor bargained on a tour full of hungover teenagers, so it was now, half an hour in, that he decided to introduce the legend of the main attraction of the various Loch cruises. He'd wake this lot up.

'Plenty of room for a monster to hide eh?' he added with a sweeping gaze over the water, vibrant ripples from the boat disrupting the perfect reflection of the sky.

'Have you ever seen anything?' asked Blake from the back of the deck, where they were all seated on weathered wooden benches, held together with three coats of green paint and rusty nails.

'Yeah!' seconded Mercia.

'As it so happens, I actually have,' replied John 'It was on a tour. We were powering down by Urquhart and we'd all just had lunch, so we were all pretty busy tidying up our mess, as you do. A wee boy asked me if we had any toilets aboard, and as I looked up to answer him I saw two parallel ripples about thirty feet away from the boat, and racing towards us,' he paused to look at their faces, which were all glinting up at him in concentration, 'Obviously I screamed like a girl.' he laughed, echoed by the group.

'But then, as quickly as.... whatever it was... had appeared, it disappeared. Luckily some of the tour saw it too and I wasn't labelled as insane. Or at least not too insane.'

'Did you get a picture?' asked Blake.

'Nah, sadly not. The one great Kodak moment of my life, and no one had a bloody camera out.'

'What do you think it was?' said Alec.

'Well, over the years there've been lots of explanations for what people think it could be. Seals, eels, waves, fish, lumps of wood. Even a giant worm. I, on the other hand, honestly don't know. I like to believe in the monster theory. The legends been around for centuries and it's interesting to think that there's something in these waters that can't be explained by modern science.'

'You say it's been around for centuries but didn't the first sightings only begin after the building of the road next to the Loch?'

'Aye, the first modern sightings. Before, the Loch was fairly remote, not easy to get to nor see. In fact, the first documented encounter with the Monster comes from the Life of Saint Columba, who was an Irish missionary in the sixth century, working in Scotland to convert the Picts to Christ. He and some of his followers came across a group of people burying a man who had been mauled to death by a 'water-beast' in the River Ness, which links to the Loch. Columba, at the protest of the group of Picts, sent one of his followers into the River, to swim and tempt the beast from hiding. When it appeared on the surface and had the swimmer within easy reach, Columba commanded in the name of God that the beast should not touch the man but go back from where it came. It stopped as if ropes had been tied around it, and then submerged. Ofcourse, everyone praised Columba and his God.'

'But haven't there been all sorts of studies done, with sonar and things that disprove the existence of a monster entirely?'

'There's been studies, and actually most of them came back with some rather strange findings. Moving objects detected of around 20 feet in length, strange wailing calls like those whales make.'

Alec eyed John incredulously.

'But yes, the most recent scanning expedition returned nothing and showed no underwater caves in Loch Ness, which is a theory that most believers put forward. However, as you'll remember from the story, St. Columba stopped a creature in River Ness. If this creature can move via rivers, then there is every chance that it does not stay in the same Loch at all times. After all, scientists have told us that there is not enough food to keep an animal of such proposed size alive in this Loch alone.'

'Right,' said Alec.

'So in other words, keep our cameras out?' smiled Blake.

'Absolutely. Just remember to tell the press which tour company you used if you do manage to get a picture!' John laughed back.

The cloud that had been over them for the duration of their trip finally began to release its hold from the sun, whose shy autumn rays now glinted on the water. The mountains rose around the Loch like the high walls of a fort, protective of their precious populace. Leo had never seen so many shades of green, nor realised how intimately the colour blue mixed with them. The loch appeared to be an enormous painter's bowl, absorbing and diluting all the tones of Gaia's brush.

'Now, coming up on your left you'll see Urquhart Castle - which is open to the public for.... oh about seven pounds I think.... and is signposted easily from Fort Augustus. However, if you just want a good picture, we'll slow when we come beside it. This castle was the scene of many.......' John continued with his tour-guide lecture, but Leo couldn't help but phase out. The castle was beautiful, ravaged by time and full of history, its half-gold stone shining like a beacon from the shore - but Leo was far more interested in the Loch. He'd seen a ripple out to the starboard side, which he'd assumed was a fish, yet every couple of minutes, with startling regularity - the same spot on the surface of the water rippled out from a point.

'......when in the 14th century....' John's voice became half clear.

Why were the ripples getting bigger? Salmon in a feeding frenzy maybe? Leo had just decided to turn his head back towards the tour guide so as not to look rude when his eye betrayed his mind.

At the spot where the ripples had been growing in larger and larger concentric rings, an enormous ink-blue reptilian head rose from the water, its slender serpentine neck following gracefully behind. As it levelled its head, two horns became visible to Leo, stretching backwards from its skull. Its eyes were as black as tar and the inside of its mouth, which it had opened to reveal a set of menacing teeth, was velvet red. Leo sat quite still, paralysed by shock and unable to shout for attention.

Then, as suddenly as the creature had surfaced, it descended by lowering its neck and head back down with a somewhat circular motion into the depths of the Loch. Leo on the other hand, remained motionless.

After a while, Isla, who was sitting next to him, noticed that something was up.

'You ok?' she said, but he stayed where he was, head twisted in the direction of where the monster had just been.

'Oi!' she nudged him 'What's up?'

Leo shook himself. The air was warmer than your average Scottish autumn and yet still, he felt freezing. They needed to get off this boat.

'Nothi..... Nothing.... I just feel a bit sick,' he strained to say as he turned to face her.

'How badly?'

'Err... pretty badly... ' It was a lie, but he didn't have to act. His fear and nausea were genuine.

'....and after having taken the castle, they sabotaged it, completely rendered it useless......' John continued in the background.

'Do you think you can handle the rest of the cruise?'

'I hope so.'

'No, no, if you feel that sick we'll get them to go back now. We can't have you being stuck out here making it worse.'

'But what about the others?'

'They'll be cool with it. Look at you.'

That wasn't exactly the answer he was expecting. Did this mean he always looked unwell? His mind raced in a desperate search for the best course of action. If he pretended to be sick, they'd be off the boat in less than an hour. If he didn't, they were still scheduled in for three. He looked at his companions and saw that their faces had brightened slightly, their hangovers wearing off thanks to the first-class scenery. No. He wouldn't wreck their plans any more than he already had. Whatever it was that he saw hadn't made itself known in the first hour of their trip, so why would it have any reason to do so in the last three. Plus, hardly anybody ever saw it. That had to be good news, and besides, if it wanted to sink the boat - Leo shivered slightly at the thought of it - it would've done so by now.

'No,' he said firmly. 'I'll be fine, really. It'll pass. It's actually gotten better in the last few minutes.'

Isla looked unconvinced. Her emerald eyes bored into his, drilling for truth.

'Hmm. Well I'm keeping an eye on you. I wouldn't be surprised if you felt sick anyway, not after last night.'

Leo wondered which part of last night she meant. In his mind it was all sickening.

'Yeah, well,' and he decided not to further the subject 'I'll be fine.'

'John,' they heard Mercia say loudly over the hum of the engine and swoosh of the wind. 'Can I ask a question?'

'Go ahead, I can't promise I'll be able to answer it though. If I can't, I'll look it up and get back to you,' replied John, smiling.

'Does the Loch have any other uses?'

'Well there aren't any nuclear deterrents cruising through its waters if that's what you mean?'

'No, no, I mean, like, does anybody get their water from it or anything?'

'Aye a few people do, but not very many. A great deal more get their electricity from it though. It acts as a massive hydro-electric reservoir. In fact, we get a great deal of our electricity from water up here -- there's so much of it,' he laughed. 'They've actually just finished building a new dam, up near Skye, one of the largest ones ever to be made. Hulking great thing, throws out so much power it's unreal.'

'That's where we're going next! Skye!' said Blake.

'Ah, you're bound to see it then, it's colossal. Really impressive,' said John, and looked at his watch, 'Anyway guys, that's me done for a while, so I'm gonna settle in for a cup o' tea and maybe a biscuit. I'll come back to you when we reach our next point of interest.' And he turned from them and walked towards the miniature cabin.

'Thanks John.'

'Yeah, cheers John,' they all offered their thanks.

'Whereabouts is Skye?' asked Leo. It was somewhere he'd heard of at least, and knew it was an island.

'Not that far away. I mean, it's a fair drive, but we're used to that by now eh?' replied Blake. 'It's North West a bit. Absolutely stunning.'

'More so than here?'

'Oh I'd say it improves on it just slightly, wouldn't you Merse?'

'Slightly's an understatement,' said Mercia.

'But she's biased, her Gran used to live there eh?'

'Aye, can't wait to go back. The Winged Isle, that's what they call it. Streams and beaches and sky.'

'Skye has sky?' said Alec.

'Oh shut up you.'

'But if it's an island how do we get to it?' asked Leo, somewhat puzzled, none of them had the money for a ferry crossing.

'A massive great bridge.' said Isla.

'Oh. Okay. Whoops.' Leo felt the blood run to his cheeks.

'We're definitely gonna need to get going more or less as soon as we get off this boat though, if that's ok by everyone? Like, no time for pit-stops or food-stops.'

'Errrmm--'

'Al, mate we can get food when we get there.'

'Aye,' sighed Alec, resolute.

'Everyone else good?'

'Mmhmm,' some of them said, the others nodded.

'Brilliant.'

There was a clanging from the cabin as John dropped a thermos and struggled to catch it against the metal sideboard.

'Hey Al, do you reckon you'd swim in this?' Blake said, reclining back further on the bench, Mercia under his arm.

'What are you on about? He'd sink,' said Isla, wearing a grin, 'Well, at least that's if his running is anything to go by. You have to actually use your muscles to swim.'

'How about I drag you in with me?' replied Alec. 'Then I'd have your enormous head to buoy me up.'

Blake ignored them and said simply, 'I wouldn't. Too risky. Wouldn't want to be Nessie chow.'

'I probably would if it were a bit shallower,' said Mercia, winding her fingers through Blake's.

'How about you Leo?' asked Blake.

'No. Never,' Leo snapped back and Blake looked hurt. 'I mean, no, like you said - too risky. We have no idea what's in there.'

'Oh nothing's in there, come off it,' said Alec, 'It's just some tourist-trap ghost story. I'd happily swim in it, just to put an end to the myth. I'd even let you lot watch me do it.'

'Not being funny, but never mind the monster - if I saw you emerge from the Loch with only your swimming kecks on I'd run for the hills screaming, telling everyone I met what a hideous beast I'd just seen,' said Isla, and they all laughed.

John never did come back out from the cabin, but they continued just like that for the rest of the cruise. By the time he came to step off the deck and on to the pier, Leo had almost forgotten all about the creature he saw, and had convinced himself he had been dreaming. After all, they were all tired. He must've fallen asleep for a second. Must have.

Normality

The hours they spent in the car rolled by for Leo, with the wilderness expanding on either side and the mountains rearing up from the ground like the fists of slaves in the hold below, cracking the decking of a vast rust-red ship. The only other inhabitants of this treeless and barren domain were the occasional pheasant, grouse and red deer, for although they were on a major road, a trunk which connected towns to towns - they never passed more than one other car on their entire journey. That is, of course, until they reached Skye. An island of immense natural beauty that was once home to a great economy and a large and thriving population, though now served as little more than a dormitory for the workers of the surrounding mainland, so Mercia told him. That and tourists.

Upon their entry to the Island the intimidating figures of the Black Cuillin towered over them like watchful grandparents, recumbent in their carpeted seats. This was the Highlands that Leo had read about in his leather-bound *Odham's* press. As they drove past them, on the road to Portree, Leo vowed to the tune of *Meatloaf's Like a Bat out of Hell* that he'd come back here one day to climb them.

No doubt lost in thoughts of their own future, the others were silent too and it was only as they passed a large and modern school building, its pupils spilling off the campus like the a beer out of a mishandled glass that conversation returned to the car.

'What!? How do these lot get away with it up here?' said Blake, perturbed, 'They're worse than I ever was - look at that tie. It might as well be a bow..... And what is that under that shirt?'

'I think it's a footie top babe,' said Mercia.

'But it's black and white! Seriously, these guys get away with it up here don't they?'

'Mate, it's probably the only school on the whole island. They've got no one else to compare themselves to. Or compete with for that matter,' said Alec.

'Still. Gits. I'd have got detention for looking like that!'

'They've finished school Blake, they're not on the grounds anymore, they can do what they like. Did you remember to pack your pipe and slippers for this trip?' said Isla.

'Aye, I seem to remember someone always wearing trainers to school,' said Mercia.

'Only so I could play fitba',' Blake said defensively, his voice a little quieter than before.

'Well, maybe he needs his team's shirt to play in.'

'Meh. Leo, you agree with me eh? You'd never've gotten away with that would you?' he caught Leo's eyes in the wing mirror.

'Our top buttons had to be done up, shirts tucked in and skirts never higher than the knee.'

'You wore a skirt?' laughed Alec.

'No, the girls I mean.'

'Well there we go guys, someone who had it stricter than us. Didn't think it was possible, but,' said Blake, completely ignoring his friend's instigation.

Leo had never really considered his school to be strict. Ridiculous: yes. 'Make-up exacerbates skin conditions' and 'Hair ties will be in school colours only.' But not strict. After all, the three major schools in the area all had the same policies, if anything his was more relaxed, so he never complained. Other than when he was ordered to stand up in class once and his Maths teacher, a horrid old troll of a woman, perched herself on his desk and fastened his top button; her face only inches away from his. They don't care if you can't breathe, or die of strangulation. Provided your corpse looks the part and is good on paper.

'Anyone else hungry?' asked Alec as they rounded the corner into the centre of Portree.

'Aye, we'll park up and grab something before we head over to Staffin,' said Blake.

'Staffin?' said Leo.

'Sorry mate, I forgot you weren't with us when we planned this trip, yeah - our port of call on Skye is a wee place called Staffin. Has brilliant beaches.'

'It's where my Gran used to live too, so there's a few people I sort of know there. We're supposed to be going to a ceilidh tonight that they're having at the local pub,' said Mercia.

'A.... a what?' Leo was utterly confused. Had she just made a word up?

'Don't worry, you'll see.'

The low sun that had been shining in through the window next to Leo, obstructing his view, retreated as Blake deftly guided his antique car into the confined parking space between two high-sides. The shadow spread across them like butter from a warm knife and Leo felt his stomach pang. It had been hours since he'd eaten.

'Right, I think I saw a mini supermarket up the hill a bit,' said Blake as he fiddled in the drivers' seat, locating all his possessions. 'Pick-a-nick time!!'

As he stepped from the car and into the open, chilly air Leo shivered slightly and crossed his arms in front of him.

'I want to get back in the car already.' said Mercia 'it's silly cold out here.'

'It's only gonna get colder, we'll be in winter before we know it,' said Isla as she rose up into a huge stretch.

Alec had found his way over to Blake, and together they began to dawdle over to the hill, leading the way for the others. Isla ran up behind Alec and poked him in the back, fixing herself into their conversation, whilst Mercia stayed behind to walk beside Leo.

'Know what you're gonna get?' she asked him.

'Not yet, probably a sandwich or something. How about you?'

She fumbled with the strap of her handbag, looking down at her chest, trying to make it even and straight and ensure it didn't ruffle her top, 'Hmmm? Oh, yeah probably the same actually. You know what we could do?' She finally satisfied herself that bag was in the right place and looked up at Leo, 'We could share a large roll, cut it in half and then share things to go in it as well. Bound to be cheaper than going it alone, especially on one of those ready-made things?'

'Yeah, definitely,' Leo liked her thinking, though he was going to get a very, very large chocolate bar as well. This pact had already been made with his stomach, and nothing was going to interfere with it.

'So what you thinking of Scotland so far?' she asked.

'Yeah, I'm really liking it actually, it's really wild and remote. There's so much walking and camping you could do up here.'

'You're gonna like tonight then.'

'Why's that?'

'The tent's coming out and we're going to be staying beside the beach.'

'Really!? I mean.... is it big enough for all of us?' He didn't want to single himself out anymore, but what he really meant was - 'is it big enough for me?'

'Uh huh, We can all fit in it and then some. There's four compartments including the "living space".'

'The tent has a living room?'

'Aye, it's pretty nice. We've used it more than hostels as it's much cheaper. I mean, even if we have to pay its at least half the cost.'

'Yeah, brilliant.' said Leo, and then a thought suddenly occurred to him 'But.. I don't have a sleeping bag.'

'That's ok. I'm sure we can sort you something out.'

'Cheers.'

The pavement was steadily inclining beneath their feet and the shops beside them passed by in flashes as they headed for their destination. Leo took a quick look around and saw that in the window of one of these shops, a large atlas of Scotland stood propped up, spotlight shining on its curved spine. Dangling from the ceiling were model boats, twisting aimlessly on varying lengths of fishing wire. Leo half expected to see a tiny seagull float through the scene or a cardboard wave to complete it, but there was nothing more than the atlas and the boats. Raising his eyes to the shop-sign he read:

Hamish Corvey -MODELS AND HOBBIES

Leo thought it an odd display for a hobby-shop, but then, his local store had had nothing but great banners plastered over the windows, preventing any eager child from seeing through without being escorted in under the watchful eyes of his parents. Much better to give a glimpse of transparency, even if it was merely an obscure taster open to all interpretations. One could be forgiven for thinking that you were looking at a tackle shop, or indeed a bookstore from this window.

Presently the door to the shop slammed as a young boy left, carrying an enormous plastic bag that seemed to dwarf his small stature. Whatever was in that bag, Leo was certain that the boy would need to stop for breath on his way home, or else collapse beneath its weight.

The impact of the closing door caused the boats in the window to bounce and swing on their cords and the spotlight to dim for a moment. The boy had, without knowing it, caused a violent tempest in the wild seas of Corvey's window. It was one that would not settle, and when the next patron came, their opening of the door would further the storm - ripple after ripple causing full movement and unrest until eventually the atlas of Scotland itself would begin to move and detach from its props.

'She likes you, you know.'

Mercia's voice dragged Leo back to reality.

'What?' he said, taken aback.

'Isla. Isn't it obvious?'

'Isn't what obvious?'

'She's really keen on you.'

'Really?' Leo looked ahead of them to Isla, who'd just flicked her hair over her shoulder and was smiling at something the boys were saying to her. He was spellbound.

'And,' Mercia's eyes traced Leo's, 'it looks like you feel the same eh?'

'What?'

'Come on, don't be shy!'

Leo's eyes fell to the floor, and readjusted to the pieces of black chewing gum that marched up the pavement like the footprints of an elf.

'It's obvious you do like her.'

'So.... so why ask then?'

'You do!? You do like her then!? Ahah!' She almost skipped.

'Shhhh,' Leo looked up at Isla ahead of them. Alec had just opened the door to the supermarket and they were walking in, 'don't tell anyone will you?'

'It's not like anyone can't see!'

'Well maybe... but... please...' he looked intently at Mercia.

'Hey, come on, I just told you that she likes you too! One of you's gotta make the first move. Or do nothing, y'know. Pretend. Either's fine,' and she skipped away ahead of him, before turning full circle.

'She's head over heels, really.' With that, she smiled broadly from ear to ear - her pretty face lost in her china teeth - and went into the supermarket, leaving Leo alone outside.

'She likes me...' he whispered as his hand grasped the door-handle. But its grip didn't last very long. The butterflies exploded inside of him and were fighting their way out. He made a fist with his right hand and then pulled his arm down and in sharply. He thought his grin would never end, that these tingling sensations would never stop, that he would always feel this light.

A customer came out of the shop, and gave him a look of incredulity. It obviously wasn't normal for young man to hang around outside shops. So he coughed, bit down hard on his lip and slipped inside the slowly closing door. Things were looking up.

The Selkie

'Well... it doesn't look too bad. I mean, I don't think it's going to fly off or anything.'

Mercia was walking backwards to allow herself a better view of their handiwork.

'It'll keep us dry if nothing else!' said Blake as he rose from a crouched position.

Though he seemed to be the only one, Leo was rather pleased with himself. They had just finished putting the tent up, which was something that he'd never done before, and there it was - pegged in on the slope of a hill, proudly waiting for occupants and unlikely to collapse.

'What time does the ceilidh start Merse?' asked Isla.

'What's the time now?'

'4.15,' said Alec, checking his watch.

'About forty-five minutes then.'

'Cool, well, now it's up - shall we head down to the beach for a bit, then get to the pub a little early?' Isla said to everyone.

'Aye, check out the competition,' said Alec.

'Like anyone's gonna out-spin me!' said Blake, 'I've won competitions for it.'

'Spin?' said Leo. They still hadn't told him what exactly a ceilidh was, and with the mention of the word 'spin' he was now picturing some disastrous drunken fair-ground ride, or at the very worst end of the spectrum an enormous hydraulically-controlled bull. Did they have those in Scotland?

'Haha! Look at his face!' said Alec.

They all smirked at each other and in Leo's general direction. Those sort of knowing, malicious smiles. He was the last turkey at Christmas. And they were Bernard Matthews. A glut of images flashed across his mind - people strapping a pint glass to their heads and spinning round, arms out like a lunatic imitating a dive-bombing aeroplane. One by one people stepping up to try their luck on an over-sized wheel of the sort you used to find on television game-shows in the nineties. Oh no, there were going to be sequins and a spry old gentleman, cadging him to bet more money and lose his dignity, only to be a shown an artificially shiny microwave being caressed by a dollybird called 'Samantha' and revolving on a silver platter. In the others' laughter he could hear the theme-tune and saw the glitzy curtains in the whites of their eyes. He opened his eyes wide in utter terror.

'You'll be fine,' said Isla through her smirk, 'Just,' she chuckled, 'don't eat too much tonight eh?'

The smatter of giggles reverberated from them and danced through the air to Leo's face like a slap.

'A ceilidh can tend to make you a bit dizzy,' said Mercia.

'Oh... right... okay,' mumbled Leo, utterly lost.

'Don't worry man, I'll go easy on you,' said Blake. 'But for now, beach?'

'Sure,' replied Leo.

'This way then.'

At the bottom of the hill was a rocky path that lead away from their impromptu campsite and trailed off behind some boulders that were nearly twice the size of Leo. For a while they simply walked, the air as still and silent as a church at midnight. On either side of them the boulders grew more numerous, and the pathway sloped at first, before rising once more to another hill. Leo let his eyes follow the careful pattern of his feet, which half-hovered over the path, divining for a safe spot, free from mud and sharp rocks. He didn't much like the quiet which seemed to crush his minds with thoughts of home, but they were ambling single file and anticipating the beach they'd heard so much about. The clouds overheard were thick and black now.

Placing foot in front of foot, Leo followed the group along the winding path, hardly allowing himself to look up from his feet for fear of falling over.

'Now *that* is a beach, eh?' said Blake up ahead as the sky stretched in front of them and opened out to panorama.

Clambering over the final steps of the rugged path, Leo allowed himself to look up. Before him was the most beautiful beach he'd ever seen. Sure he'd seen pristine white sands and water as clear as glass. Yes, he'd seen places with nothing but miles of endless turquoise ocean on the horizon. But to Leo, in that moment, they all paled in comparison. The sand which crept from the sea and cushioned the boulders that surrounded them, now they'd crossed the brow, was as black as night. It was as if the Gods, in a moment of fury, had plucked one of the storm clouds above and draped it on the shore as a punishment for outshining the beauty of the sun. There it was, prisoner for all eternity, guarded by the ferocious waves which crashed upon a ring of rocks that sheltered their natural harbour.

As he stepped out further on to the beach, the wind bit at his ankles and sent his hair in all directions.

'This is gorgeous!' shouted Isla over the sounds of the sea and the wind and she gave Leo a little grin before sending herself into a child-like twirl. The subtle intensity of the blue light illuminated her and, as she spun, she seemed to shine, her vibrant hair swinging out from her head like a halo.

'What nutter do you think lives over there?' said Alec, pointing towards an island a fair way offshore where a sort of dwelling could just be made out.

'I'm not sure anybody does live over there mate,' said Blake, 'look closer at it. It seems a little bit ragged.'

'And there's no boat,' said Isla, 'You definitely couldn't live there without a boat.'

'Maybe they're out,' offered Alec.

'Nah, come on, *look* at the place man, it's nae more than a shack. Some old radge probably uses it for drying his fish catch. That or smoking them.'

'I don't know so much.'

'Would *you* live out there alone?' asked Isla.

'Aye, I would, as it happens.'

'You'd never.'

'Can't think of anything better.'

''Til you drown that is.' said Blake.

'No, I .....'

'Where's Mercia?'

By now the group had wandered far along the beach and were standing almost at the water's edge.

'Ah! There she is!' cried Blake.

And there she was. On the opposite side to the path where they'd joined the beach there ran a significant wedge of rock at sand level. In deep gouges that had formed over the years, there still lay water - rock pools. It was over one of these rock pools that Mercia was crouched, evidently deep in thought.

'You alright Merse?' called Isla.

'Yeah, yeah, I think I've just found something my Gran was telling me about. You guys should check it out!'

'I hope it's not a starfish,' said Alec derisively as they made their way towards her.

'Who knows mate,' said Blake, 'You alright Leo?'

'Yeah, yeah fine thanks, just enjoying the scenery.'

'Ah, ok, you just seem abit quiet is all.'

'Nah, I'm just tired if I'm honest.'

Catching this sentence, Isla shot him a look and he quickly covered his tracks.

'Never road-tripped before. Taking a lot out of me,' he laughed.

'Aye, I get you.'

Leo knew he was being quiet, but it wasn't out of rudeness or any particularly pertinent feelings of hurt. If anything he felt inert and it was vastly easier and vastly more entertaining to allow others to do the talking. He was due to lead a life sitting on the sidelines: why act any different now?

'Look at these...' said Mercia, raising herself up as they reached her.

'What? The rock-pools?' said Alec without even looking down.

'No, genius........ *look,*' and she put her foot into an impression in the rock. 'Dinosaur footprints.'

'Ah, wow!' they all exclaimed.

'Yeah, my Gran told me a while back how someone had come across them at low tide. They're supposed to be the footprints of some huge herbivore!'

Leo's heart had lurched at the mention of the word 'Dinosaur'. It was better to pretend that they didn't exist, had never existed. He hadn't seen anything and wouldn't again.

'So they were here all this time and some-one's only just found them?' said Isla.

'Apparently. This beach is fairly, what's the word?, unimportant.'

'Well it must be important to that guy on the island!' said Alec.

'No, what I meant was - there are loads like it, all over Skye.'

Leo, like most of them, had zoned out by now. Him especially as those footprints of Whateverasaurus only served to remind him of the semi-impossible he kept encountering. He wondered how easy it was to damage the brain.

Having left the footprints some time ago, his eyes had been resting on the horizon, where the storm clouds were gathering like a swarm of insects. Unaware of what was closing in on them, the waves lapped gently on the shore, humming a comforting tune with pleasant regularity. This constant ebb and flow soothed his mind and calmed his thoughts - much like watching goldfish swim in an endless loop around their tank. He was freed from the shackles of the whirring worries that defined him and basked in temporary contention, aware of nothing but the drone of familiar voices and the wind skipping through his hair.

He let his imagination run wild and saw before him, readying to land, an armada of Norse longboats, their single sails carrying their deadly cargo eagerly towards the tar-black land. His heart quickened as he felt the passengers' adrenalin; fear, excitement and determination coursing and clashing within his every pore, each fighting desperately for domination.

'What do you think Leo?'

'Wha.... wha?'

'Do you reckon that Isla looks most like a Dinosaur out of all of us?' asked Alec.

Ever closer they urged, their sails precipitating the plunder of the shores by enslaving the wind. Their hacked-out, dark wooden hulls cast shadows like the first drips of ink into water, spreading like a false idea - rejecting all truth within its darkness and clinging desperately to its origin. Though it were but rough-hewn interpretation, on it surged. Ever closer.

A clap of laughter brought his eyes back into focus and just as the ship appeared; they dissolved. No more than a slither of a memory. All that was, except for the shadow of the lead ship, which continued its march towards the shore. Leo blinked hard twice, thinking he must have got something in his eye. But sure enough, each time he opened them, there the shadow was. Or at least, it *looked* like a shadow. But then, why was it circular? Why was it –

'Oh!' he chortled, clearly he hadn't missed anything of importance. 'No, I don't know, I wouldn't say-'

'OH GUYS LOOK!' squealed Mercia as she jumped to her feet and edged towards the sea, pointing erratically.

'Look at what, Merse?'

'What're you on about?'

Just then, not an arm's length from where Mercia's hand was pointing, a black head with enormous, glossy eyes broke the surface of the puddle-light and cast its gaze over the group. Seconds later, it re-submerged.

'It's a seal!!' Mercia screamed, when the head returned, a few feet closer and a couple of hands further to the left.

For a while they all stood, enraptured by the presence of this stranger. Whilst most of them had seen seals and suchlike before, most of them had seen them in zoos; behind the safety of six inch plexiglass and barbed wire. The manic shades of the safety signage, emblazoned with a severed, bitten hand loomed over their heads and sanitised their experience. For them, this was like the first time they'd been in their gardens and marvelled at the birds simply being there - for doing as they wished. The illusion of Man's control over Nature shattered in the time it took for a bird to descend onto the chemically manicured lawn. A surge of vulnerability accompanied by solid fascination and (in their innocent minds, free from want) a deep set veneration like the strum of a deep bass within your chest.

The seal, shadow-black and only slightly more solid, eyed them fervently from one position and then returned below, only to rise a few feet away. Like a swimming rounders fielder it was constantly reassessing how close was too close.

When the last streams of the sun shone pink across the woodsmoke clouds, their visitor submerged his final time. Leo looked across to Isla in the fading light, and saw that she had her arms folded across herself, trembling slightly. The very tips of her lips had turned a pastel blue and her face was flushed. Her hair danced nonchalantly in the wind and for all the world she was an Ice Queen. Yet she was still a warmth to him.

'Hey, it's getting pretty cold out here guys, shall we head off?' he said, burying his eyes deep into the sand.

'Aye,' replied Alec. 'Top seal that, but when I'm cold and hungry - I need to leave.'

'Are you ever not hungry mate?' quipped Blake.

Alec stayed silent and took a few steps towards the rocks that led to the campsite. They all followed, but as they did, Blake pulled Leo to the back.

'Not sure I should've said that.'

'But doesn't Isla say it all the time?'

'Aye, and I think it's getting to him more than he lets on to her.'

'Oh.'

'Still, he must be superhuman. I'm very rarely actually hungry. I eat because I know have to.'

Leo considered this for a while, considering it an absurd statement.

'Anyway,' Blake continued, holding the last syllable a while, 'what's happening with you and Iz, then?'

Great. This situation again.

'Oh,' he felt his face warm despite the chill wind, 'er, n-nothing I guess.'

'Eh? Nothing? But I heard you liked each other?'

'Well, I, er, I guess we do- atleast, according to Mercia she likes me too.'

'So?'

'So what?'

'So, why the hell has nothing gone on? She must be dying with anticipation.'

'Well, it's not as simple as all that is it?'

'What do you mean? Trust me, I know Iz. She's raving about you.'

'You think so?' Two people couldn't possibly get this wrong.

'Aye, I mean, for one, I *know*. However, it's also stark raving obvious!'

Leo looked at him, and there was a glint in his eye. They were smiling too - alongside his mouth. So it was true. But now what? He couldn't just walk over to her, tell her he liked her and go in for a kiss. No, never. He wished she didn't like him. This was far worse than disappointment. He could feel his stomach squirming; a tightness in his throat; his face frozen.

'Come on buddy! What's wrong!?'

But Leo couldn't reply, he looked on ahead at the mess of red hair, scrunched up his eyes and shook his head.

'Hey,' Blake said, and shook Leo's shoulder. 'It's easy - just talk to her. Everything else follows naturally. She doesn't bite. At least not this early.' He grinned. 'I promise.'

'Yeah, it's not that I haven't-'

'Naw, I didn't mean that.'

'I know you didn't, I mean, it's just, I really don't want to wreck this now.'

'Oh don't be radge. If anything you'll be improving things. She's already tense thinking you aren't interested.'

'Really?'

'Yes mate, honest-like.'

Leo took a long, deep breath inwards and then smiled at Blake. 'Come on, let's catch them up.'

'Ah, he's keen *now*.'

'Shut up.' Leo laughed, and they started a jogging pace to join the others.

The gathering clouds of the coming storm had crept across the sky, blotting the little boy blues of the sun's fading light with a blindness. Beneath this, the heaven's rage, Poseidon's charge became a mirror, and the waves broke across each other like the lash of whip on slave. Not three feet back from the beach, as yet untouched by the elemental argument, a dark face with glassy eyes laid upon the swell. Its eyes followed the boy with golden hair and chalk-white skin. He was walking with the other humans, interacting with them. Heading towards a settlement. In one blink of those enormous eyes, the boy and the humans he was with had disappeared. When a flash lit up the clouds both above and below the ocean, so, too, did the shadow.

*

After years of neglect, the much-loved wallpaper in the bar of the *Covenanter* had begun to curl and crinkle upon itself, falling at a glacial pace towards the parquet floor. The printed scene, in black, white, and the yellow of tobacco and time, though repeated across the wall now told a different story across the curls. Time, the solemn sour sister of Decay had laid her silent hand across the once-proud prints. Where there had been a dog, a sprightly hound with perked-up ears and an active posture - there now rested a paper shelf of gathered dust. Ashes to ashes, so do we all return. His master, whose pistol once held God to ransom, searching the ceiling for an inken duck, was now bent double; his gun a crutch.

The sofa set against this wall, an old chesterfield, ripped and scarred, was the best seat in the place. The flickers of the fire reflected in the aged leather and should you settle here on a deep midwinters night, your feet outstretched towards the hearth, the wind would whip around and about the building and an hour become a minute with three blinks and a miss.

Beside the fire sat a bearded old man on a wooden stool. He was adding wood the fire and striking it rhythmically with an iron poker.

'So how far out did you say he was again?'

The group sat opposite the fire, Leo, Isla and Alec on the sofa, Mercia and Blake on stools either side.

'Not far at all,' said Mercia. 'I could see his eyes, and parts of his mottling.'

'Inquisitive little beggars, they are eh? You know it's not unheard of for there to be a whole group do that to you. They'll even follow you down the beach.'

'Aren't they scared of people, then?' asked Blake.

'No, not in the slightest. I mean, well, I don't know about all seals, but up here in these islands, they're mental. Sort of like people-' He paused abruptly, and hung his poker on the brass keeper. Then, turning to them, he said: 'In fact, there's a story about that.'

'What? About what?' asked Alec.

'Any of yous ever heard of *Selkies?*'

Silence spread through the room but for the constant crackle of the fire.

'Ah'll take that as a no then.' He reached for the top of the mantelpiece and took a long draught of his thick and murky pint. 'A long time ago now, on this very island, there lived a man by the name of Angus - a fisherman by trade. Now, he was an ambitious young man, our Angus, and he spent a considerable length of time longer out at sea than the other men. Had to get the biggest catch he did.' He took another long swig of his drink, before placing it down on the hearth.

'One night, he stayed out well past sunset, in pitch darkness he lowered and raised his nets. Before he knew it, the very first rays were beginning to light up the sky. So he thinks to himself: "I must've tripled my catch by now. Perhaps I should get home for a few hours' kip before I head to the market." So off he sets. When he reaches the harbour, he ties up his boat with haste, you know, finishes all the usual jobs, very much looking forward to his bed by now, what comes over the lapping of the waves but the unmistakable sound of laughter. Of course, at first, he decides his mind must be playing tricks on him, it was late, he was sleep-deprived; it was most likely a gull. But there it comes again. He knew his brain wasn't so fuddled as to hear something which wasn't there twice. Now, as I'm sure you can imagine, the community he lives in is very small - and, well, curiosity overtakes him. He wonders who else could possibly be up at that time in the morning, never mind enjoying themselves so much. So he goes off to look for the revellers.

'Following the sound of the laughter, he comes to a beach secluded from the harbour by some large rocks. He tiptoed towards them, and concealed himself behind one. What he saw on that beach, between a gap in the rocks, took his breath away. There, in the pale pink light of the sunrise, danced seven of the most beautiful women he'd ever seen. Their eyes were as black as night and their hair was thick, long and a shimmering shade of gold. Their skin, though warmed by the sunlight was whiter than mountain snow.

'Our friend Angus, being well-versed in the tales of these Islands and the age old knowledge from which they came; recognised immediately that these were not only strangers. They were no ordinary women. That he knew this had little to do with the fact that they were dancing, nor by the colour of their eyes, hair and skin but by the fact that these women were naked from head to toe. Laying on the rocks that formed his hide were seven soft-grey skins. These illicit dancers, porcelain beauties twirling on the sand were *Selkies* - mysterious seal-folk with the power to shed or wear their seal pelts, changing form at will.

'The longer Angus watched them dance, the harder it became for him to leave. He could not, as much as he tried, take his eyes off of one of these women, having never seen anything so lovely in his life.'

Leo felt his eyes flick sideways for an instant, then lowered them to the floor.

'Some time passed before, one by one, the Selkie women began to retrieve their skins from the rock, resume their seal form, and return to the waves. Consumed with passion, Angus couldn't bear the thought of never seeing his favourite again, and when she, the last to leave, walked towards the rock to get her skin, Angus scrambled out from his hiding place and gathered up her skin in his arms. With anguished cries the other Selkies, now in seal form, retreated from the shore, aware that there was nothing they could do. Angus told his favourite that he was going to take her home and make her a home and make a life with her. The Selkie woman cried, pleading with him to let her return to the sea, her home, but Angus wouldn't allow it. So the woman went with Angus to his village, aware that without her skin she could never return to her seal form and was trapped; his prisoner.

'For three long weeks, Angus kept the skin beside his chest, as arrangements for the wedding were made. When these were up, he wrapped the skin in cloth and hid it beneath his barn, knowing that she would never find it.

'Years passed and though the two were never rich, Angus' ambition secured them a comfortable life. With the benefit of a female hand, his house had become a home and they had three happy, healthy bairns. Though with time, the Selkie woman had come to respect Angus and loved her children, she never once forgot her home and would often walk alone to the beach and stare longingly for hours into the waves, wishing with all her might to see her friends bobbing up and down in the surf. But by far her strongest despair was the thought of her husband and children. She had already been married - to a Selkieman - when Angus took her. For hours she would sit beneath a moonlit sky and cry, one tear falling for every time she wished to see her home again; the place where she had been truly happy.

'One morning, whilst she was cooking for the day ahead, their youngest bairn came running in to her, shouting about how he'd found something, and asking what it was. It was grey, he said, and wrapped in an old cloth. Her heart jumped into her chest. Calmly she asked him what the bundle smelled like. "Like the sea ma'."

'That evening, Angus came home from work to find all the children asleep in bed and a vat of soup warm and ready on the stove for him. Patiently he walked through his house, calling out for his wife. When there was no reply, and she was nowhere to be seen, he grew fearful. With all rooms checked, he tore out of his house and ran to the barn, to look for the secret he buried all those years ago. There it was, beside the torn wooden slats of the barn floor, the filthy bundle of cloth, torn open and empty.

'Neither Angus, nor his children ever saw her again. And through the long nights, he would often be found, standing beside the shore, grieving for his lost love, and his perfect life.'

For a few moments, the Storyteller gazed into middle-distance, the flame of passion ripped from his now-dead eyes. It was only when he raised his glass and cocked his head back to drain the last of his pint that any of the group dared to speak.

'Wow, so you believe that all seals are able to change their form?' asked Mercia.

'Eh, no,' said the Storyteller, plonking his now empty glass atop the mantelpiece. 'Only some seals are Selkies but it is virtually impossible to tell the difference. Only rarely does their behaviour give it away. But, ultimately, it is wise to treat all seals with respect. Well, according to legend that is. I, myself, don't believe in it. But they *are* bloody fiesty critters!'

'Anything that encourages respect for nature can only be a good thing, eh?' said Isla.

'Oh, course. Say, guys, it was nice meeting yous like, but I really better be away before the festivities start. I'm not one for dancing.' A schoolboy smile crossed his lips, revealing small, sharp teeth.

'Oh, no, you should stay,' said Mercia, 'You don't have to dance.'

'Naw, it's alright, thanks very much. I really do have to be away.' He rose from his stool and ambled sidewards towards the door. 'Bye all.'

'Bye,' they all said.

'What a cool old guy,' said Blake, standing up and stretching.

'Cool?' said Alec, raising an eyebrow.

'Well,' Blake laughed, 'I liked him.'

'You're forever meeting strange people in pubs though. Remember that belly-dancer in Glasgow?'

'Ah, come on now - she was a *catch*!'

'Oh yeah, possibly the only belly-dancer in the world who has to use her *hands* to move her belly. I'm surprised they let her in for the price of one person.'

'I'll have you know Gisele was an incredibly talented mover.'

'Aye. In water, like the other hippos.'

'When was this!?' demanded Mercia.

'Oh, don't worry babe, I wasn't likely to run off with her.' He went to put his arm around Mercia.

'Only because you didn't have a fork-truck to hand.'

Presently they all collapsed into hysterics, and in the midst of their laughter a small, thin old woman, floated into the room and projected a mouse-like voice over them.

'For those of you taking part,' she said, 'the ceilidh is about to begin.'

'Ah! Excellent!' cried Mercia, leaping from her seat and followed the lady out of the room, flashing the others a face crushed with excitement. 'Well, come on then!'

They all rose, and like fresh infantry marching to the front line, followed behind her, stiff-limbed. Leo filed along beside Blake, watching his not-so-nimble feet and fervently hoping that his drink would work its magic.

'You ready for this?' asked Blake.

'Er, yeah, just about.'

Leo hadn't danced in public since he was ten. And then it was at school discos, where the only audience consisted of his own year-group and the ladies minding the rag-tag tuck shops in the canteen. He wondered in horror what this dancing was going to entail. He'd seen an old VHS of *Riverdance* once and had since had the concept of 'Scottish dancing' tied to that particular troupe. Stepping across the threshold of the main hall and noticing the distinct absence of any blue costumes he felt immediately relieved.

The hall was lit like a cinema theatre, darkness flirting with light. Comfort and age beamed from every surface. Panelled walls and chintzy carpet. Atop the carpet stood various tables and chairs, upholstered in the same unique fabric. Their presence proved soothed Leo's twingeing nerves, aware now that no-one was expected to stand the whole night.

At the far end of the hall was a stage which ran the length of the wall. On its plain black surface was assembled a musical band consisting of one woman holding an accordion and two men. The woman had thick, black hair, cropped close to the ear and was busily chatting away to the group, half-swivelled on the stool that supported her. The two spot-lights suspended over the stage gave them an air of the ethereal - beings of smoke set in place to be worshipped on their altar.

Stretching out in front of the stage like a pier in the mass sea of old carpet, was a dance-floor of parquetry like the ones favoured by village halls and school buildings. Gathering on this now were the willing participants of the ceilidh, clustering together gaily, drink in hand, stealing occasional glances at the band; eager not to miss the first stirrings of performance.

Taking his lead from the others, Leo left his drink and belongings at a large table, and pigeon-stepped to the dance-floor. The atmosphere in the room was a palpable strain of anticipation, inbred with the jovial conviviality so often found in the events of close communities.

When the woman with the close cropped hair was satisfied with the occupancy, she lifted up her freestanding microphone and half-whispered with the raspy voice of a heavy smoker.

'Hello all, and welcome again to this week's ceilidh. As ever, I'm Morag and I'll be your caller for the evening....'

'What's a caller?' asked Leo.

'They tell you which type of dance we will do to the music. They also teach you,' Blake replied.

'......w, I have to ask, has everyone here been to a ceilidh before?'

'Noooooooo!' came a shout from the corner furthest from the group.

Leo was glad he wasn't the only one. He imagined if he'd have been the only one needing lessons in a room full of people; a fate a million times worse than public speaking.

'Aye, OK, right,' said Morag, 'So well take it easy for the first few then.' She shifted her wait on her seat and glanced down at her accordion. 'First thing's first. Let's have you partnered up. Lads, find yourselves a lass. If there's a shortage then decide between your couple who'll be the woman.'

Immediately the mass shuffling began to find a partner. Naturally, Blake took Mercia, and all the married couples chose each other. Leo looked around the room hesitantly. Where was there a 'free' girl? He stood on his tiptoes to see over the heads of some tall local men and nearly lost balance when he felt the warmth of a hand on his shoulder.

'Hey,' said a soft voice behind him. He spun round on his feet and was astonished to find Isla standing so close to him. 'What're you looking over there for?'

Leo didn't know what to make of this question. Why wasn't Isla with Alec, everybody else had partnered up. They should be taking their places by now.

'I was, I was, just, er, looking to see if there were any girls on their own.'

'What for?'
'Well, 'cause I am.'
'Well now you're not.'
'Huh? What? Aren't you dancing with Alec?'
'No, he asked me and I told him no. I pick my own partners.'
'Oh! So, so, who's he with now?'
'Some leggy blonde.' She pointed towards the stage. 'Look.'

She was right. Leo followed the invisible line made by her pointed finger towards Alec, and there ,beside him, stood a tall girl in a tight-fitting dress with waist-length blonde hair. Though they were quite a distance apart, Leo could see why Alec had chosen her. Her striking face was drawing the eyes of all the men in the room.

'Are you gonna dance with me then?' said Isla.

'Yes!' Leo half-shouted, causing Isla to raise her eyebrows in shock. 'I mean, yeah, sure. I don't know the moves or anything, but...'

'That's okay, she'll teach us. I'm a bit rusty anyway.' She smiled the way that made Leo's insides constrict.

'Right, good, good,' came the Caller's voice above the rabble. 'Now I'm going to need all of you to spread out - for the first one - if we make a circle around the floor. Couples, if you can make sure you're an arms' length away from your neighbours.'

Smiles resonated around the room as everyone found their places, half-knocking into each other in their urgency.

'Good, good, that's great everyone. Now, the first dance we shall have tonight will be the *Gay Gordons*. For the benefit of those who have not previously been to a ceilidh, we'll have a slowed down introduction. So, Gents, if you stand to the left of your Ladies, and take their right hand with yours.'

There was a big kerfuffle as everyone hurried to obey the caller. She let them move into position, scanning the room with her eyes, and them falling on to one couple nearest to her said:

'No, no!' she laughed, 'put your arm around her back!'

The couple turned various shades of rouge, and quickly corrected themselves before waiting for the next instruction.

'Now, Ladies, take hold of the left hand of your partner with yours.'

Leo looked down at Isla, and watched her breathe. He thought she might as well be stealing his very own breath from his lungs, in order to begin a collection of life-forces, for his blood already wished to escape from his veins, surging upwards in ever-increasing doses since he'd taken her hand in his.

The Caller explained the steps, and each couple had two turns in which to practice at a slow speed without the music.

Leo laughed as Isla guided him through each sequence, as if she were a patient mother teaching her baby to walk. She would look into his eyes and count out loud '1,2,3.....' corresponding to the movement of their feet. He followed her lead, and found himself counting aloud, each number searing a different movement to his memory.

'Ok, everyone ready?' said the Caller, 'Right.... back into positions please, and we'll have a go full-step.'

The room was filled with muffled whispers and laughter, the booming voices of men incapable of quiet adding a bass tone to the busy rhythm every now and again. The caller, satisfied her crowd were in position, turned to look at her fellows and on struck the music.

For the first few beats they were quite still, listening intently for the notes that signalled their start. The nerves, though dulled by the few drinks he'd had, were standing on edge within Leo and a butterfly was fighting from its chrysalis inside his stomach. Its stirring made him feel sick, and he kept reminding himself that it wasn't a theatrical show. If he made a mistake, a mistake was made and could be rectified. That was all. No one would notice. Other than Isla. She would notice but, he hoped, she would not care. He could only hope.

Suddenly the room sprang into action, as everyone heard the gunfire to the race, a note indefinable to untrained ears. A silent signal that began the madness. Were it not for Isla, Leo would have stood for some seconds, blissfully unaware of the movement around him. But as it was, she pulled him forwards and into the first sequence.

Just as he thought, he had forgotten the correct order of the moves, and as such was not keeping in time to the music. For their first two sequences, Leo and Isla danced a style more in the manner of a half-drunk gamekeeper that had seized the front paws of his long-suffering hound and proceeded to twirl it around the parlour to a badly slurred tune. The dog would likely have been more graceful than Leo, even whilst battling to remain upstanding. Yet Isla was a natural tutor, and slowly, by the third round, everything began to fall into place. They started to synchronise to the other couples, and Leo felt the music guide him to the next step, an audible recipe for a perfect icing.

Whether it was the fault of the alcohol, intensifying his emotions with its uncaring hand, or something greater, Leo could not tell. But once he'd gotten the hang of it, and all the couples were moving as one, each playing their individual and important part in the wheel, he was euphoric. His heart lightened and lifted to such an extent that he didn't want to let go of Isla's hand for fear of floating to the ceiling. He was a part of something, connected in a way he'd never been before. He was keenly aware that, should he break off, the circle would be incomplete and fail to function - with Isla stranded alone. In this frame of mind, where the boundaries between himself and others were blurred beyond compare, spinning Isla like a ballerina inside a music box left him dazed and dizzy with her beauty radiating into him and her smile a virus infecting his lips.

The trouble with all good things though, is that they must come to an end. So it was with a final flourish, the musicians finished their tunes and all the dancers cheered and clapped. There was a bustle as many of the revellers hurried over to their groups of shy and seated friends, desperate to persuade them to take part; to become part of the circle. To feel the unification. For the most part, those friends remained unconvinced and the room wore a new uniform of disappointed faces. That is, all except the dancers who had remained on the floor, those who, like Leo and Isla, had been following the Caller's new instructions.

'The next dance will be a..........'

'That was something eh?' half-shouted Alec, who'd come to stand beside them.

'This involves standing in two separate lines....'

'My poor wee lassie couldn't handle another!'

'Lads, if you take your positions closest to the stage....'

'Hey, Leo, do you mind if I steal Isla for this one? I'll give her back, but it's been a long time since I've spun her silly.'

Isla's eyebrows raised and she looked expectantly at Leo.

'Er, no, of course not,' replied Leo. Well, what else could he say? 'No, actually I don't want you to dance with your friend because I rather like her and I'm afraid you'll steal her away.'

'Sweet. Shall we?' said Alec and he mock bowed towards Isla.

'Fine, but I'm telling you now, if you launch me into anyone you won't be wearing clothes for the rest of this trip.'

'Oh aye?!'

Isla shot him a look of contempt, 'Don't even.... Ugh.'

Leo hovered for a moment as they each parted from his company, following the word of the Caller and falling into line. Soon though, the rung-less ladder of partners had stretched not only out in front of him, but around him. This was perhaps the right time to leave the dance-floor and watch from the relative comfort and safety of a carpet-upholstered chair.

Still, even as he reached the table and clasped gently at his pint of beer, the condensation moist and cool on his too-warm fingers, his eyes refused the leave the floor. They were drawn by some magnetism to Isla, and the room phased out, his whole focus on her. The harsh artificial lights threw shadows on her face, rendering her now a painting, now a print, always a work of art.

It occurred to Leo that watching the dances play out, whilst pleasantly entertaining and convivially uplifting, held no candle to the ecstatic witchcraft that held you bound in step, time, and rapture during participation. He busied himself with thoughts of a future that took no account of the past; he thought of Isla beside him in white. He thought of a woodland, grounds, and a humble stone home of his own. His trouble was that he divined as she danced, a shadow on the surface of the scrying bowl, a world apart from the one he had. To dream, to allow himself to imagine all those things was to forsake both their lives in exchange for smoke. To believe that she would love an orphan, a damaged and over-sensitive soul, when she was ablaze with the inferno of life and destined for higher places.

*

'Go on! That's it!' laughed a boy maniacally.

'Get..........off.......' said another boy, paler than the other children around him.

'What do you think I should do with him?'

'Spit in his face!' screamed the laughing boy.

'Nooo.... ummmm....' cried the pale boy.

From behind the wall the children shouted and laughed with glee at the spectacle taking place before them. Their eldest friend, two years above the rest, had pinned down a pale blonde boy on the lawn in the front garden of one of their houses that was separated from the street by nothing but a low cement wall. The boy lived round the corner from them. They were his friends.

'Alright!' said the older boy as he twisted his face into a cruel smile, his eyes gleaming with malice and fixed upon his victim.

'Noooo!!!!' shouted the pale boy, writhing beneath the older boy's grip. He was desperate. He managed to free one of his arms from the ground, only for it to be slammed just as quickly back in place and sending a sharp jolting pain through him and his eyes filled with tears.

Through the haze he saw the older boy's look of glee and knew he was helpless. He looked across the wall, and saw his friends standing there smiling, jeering, entranced. He closed his eyes and prepared for the inevitable. He knew in that moment what friendship was.

*

The room felt as if it was closing in around Leo, encasing him in the moment as the warmth he felt in his stomach expanded. It didn't matter that he was sat at a long and empty table. He wasn't alone. The tempo of the dance had rapidly increased and he watched, beaming, as his friends slipped and twirled around each other. A couple of tourists had joined in by this point, attempting to learn the steps as they went along, which given the late hour entailed a lot of staggering in the wrong direction: but even this couldn't spoil the general mood. Whenever they went wrong, the other dancers merely pointed them in the right direction.

When the music finally stopped, the meticulous order and sense of place and purpose evaporated, leaving the scores of dancers stranded at their last step and lost amongst a throng. For a fraction of a second there was silence, a manifestation of shock as if a summer's day had immediately given way to snow. Then the steady trickle of applause began to seep through the crowd, becoming a wave whistled over by a wind of half-lark cheers. As the surf swelled and broke, Leo lost sight of his companions who were floating centrally - somewhere.

Lifting his drink to his lips, Leo gazed on - a half smile still plastered on his face. The sweet bitterness of social lubricant found his tongue and dowsed his scorched throat with the crisp relief of rain on a hot day. He drank on. Eager. There was a magic to this serum. One could be anything and he could be a man. He would tell Isla. Then what? He didn't care. Everything would be fine. Everything would ....

The dancefloor was clearing, couple by couple, group by group. And as heat reveals the lemon's ink, letter by letter his friends were revealed to him. His friends. His. There, embraced like two writhing snakes; the apple long-since rotten, were Isla and Alec sealed in a kiss and the truth laid bare. His insides compressed, tightened hard to form a knot and a nausea surged upwards to his throat. His eyes burned and the smile melted from his face. Without a word, he slammed the glass back on the table and rose to leave. The pub was now packed and navigating his way to the door was a challenge that saw him breathing in to squeeze between gaggles of inebriated Scotsmen, his shoulder knocking into pints and short glasses. The air was thick with the stench of booze, bodies and just-burnt fags. The more he pigeon-stepped towards the door the more Leo felt the need to be outside as his nausea consolidated its gains up his gullet and was pushing for the final conquest. He was going to make it. Charging into a run, he forced his way through the entrance hall, sending a short old man flying into the coat-rack, thrust himself through the heavy door and out into the icy night air.

Hitting him like a smack in the face, the cold night slowed him to a dawdle, made him acutely aware of the vultures, lurking beneath their hunched wings; fumes emanating from their mouth. The deep scarlet flickers and their callous black eyes pierced him and he picked up his pace once more. The street flashed past him and the buildings were no more than shapes, twisting and moulded into one long block of dismal colour. By the time he arrived at the wall, the defensive wall that bordered the beach, he was already coughing and spluttering - a hostage to his constitution.

Some moments later, he pushed himself up from the wall and wiped his mouth carelessly with the back of his hand. He had nowhere to go. He was stuck hundreds of miles from home; what had been home. So instead he staggered onwards. He'd distance himself from them. From everyone. The wretched streetlights only intensified his malady and became a catalyst; pushing him along.

For some time he advanced like a sailboat, tacking his zigzag course down the beachfront. The gap between himself and the lights of town grew ever greater and the few buildings that appeared on his route now were blacked out: mere silhouettes of civilisation. Still his stomach churned. Soon, however, the drink in his system showed itself as a leaden weight and he grew tired.

With the wall at an end long behind him, he'd been walking beside rocky mounds that obscured his view of the sea and obliterated his sense of direction. Ahead of him, a path forked from the road and penetrated through the first gap in that he'd seen in the otherwise barricade-like elevations. The path bore every sign of neglect, its lumber markers having half collapsed like the pillars of Stonehenge and the vegetation creeping ever further on to the way. The closer Leo came to the path, the more obvious it was that it had been a rambler's entrance down to the seafront. To a beach. The trail of half-sand stretched on into the night until it was enveloped by darkness. Where the road continued, the solitary street guardians lit up the way with their dismal glow, no doubt marching with statue-speed to the next bastion of habitation.

So Leo, spotting a chance to be alone, seized the opportunity firmly and stumbled without hesitation into the abyss.

It was not long before his eyes adjusted to the grim light levels, though he could still only see little more than shadows. He stopped only once in the passage. Raising his eyes to the sky, he had hoped to have glimpse of stars. No such luck was to be had though, as the night sky had sheathed itself with cloud - a prudent measure, Leo thought; after all, the more frequently you see even the most magnificent of sights, the more they lose their fascination and are reduced to background noise. Otherwise, with the wind whipping at his heels, he pressed on.

The first betrayal of the sea's presence sent a crashing wave of recollection through Leo. An ethereal onslaught that had him cycle in a time-warped fashion through his life to-date. He was 3, wearing red underpants and holding a matching spade; he was 5, hunting critters and creatures in rock-pools in a far-off land; he was 14 and reclining on a lounger, brushing sand from his legs. He shook his head and exhaled the bittersweet salt air out through his flared nostrils. Its fresh scent had formed yet another memory - albeit one that perhaps wouldn't last beyond the morning's hangover.

At this point the path dropped off sharply into an almost vertical ridge and Leo slipped, landing flat on his back and clutching awkwardly at the ground: now almost completely sand. He recoiled in disgust whilst pulling himself back on to his feet, as his hands grasped the trailing roots of plants inside the loose mass of sand. There was nothing quite like that feeling. He continued to make his way down the shifting surface like a fleck of stone inside an hourglass. During one of his many stops - taken to plan his route - he heard with clarity the rattling and groaning of the night-time sea. Suddenly he no longer felt alone. He'd walked into Poseidon's bed-chamber. He heard the deep rasps of breath tear across the waves and he was content. He wasn't alone. He wasn't in company either. Unfortunately this imbued him with a little too much confidence and in the next step, before he knew it, Leo was tumbling face first at full speed down the hill.

'Ahhhhhhhhhhhhhhhhhhhhhhhhhhhhhhhhhhhhhhhhhh !' he yelled as he was thrown from ramp to ramp, pebbles and ragged stones cushioning his landing and bruising his bruises.

He came to a halt with a dull thud and a face full of beach. Spitting and coughing he pushed himself up and shook himself violently, trying to expel the particles of half-glass from his eyes.

Piece by piece but still in blur, his sight returned. Black gave way to black. Black to blue and grey. To grey and navy and shimmering white. And now he was there he had no plan. What next? He was no Robinson Crusoe. He couldn't very well operate-his-way-round-a-till out of trouble. He stood quite still, balancing his weight on one foot and stared, lamb-like at the shore. His legs eventually revolted and carried him of their own accord to a spot not a few feet away from the water and then withdrew their balance in an act of defiance, leaving him sat, quite upright; legs in a diamond.

As Leo began to shiver, his eyes open in a dewy slit, the sinister darkness invaded his brittle mind. Maleficent conjurations danced upon the water. Jacob, dressed in his football kit and chasing after a ball; the long avenue of trees on the common, swaying in the summer breeze; an open book, full of handwriting; Isla laughing, her crimson hair defying gravity.

He ran his fingers through his hair and shifted his unsure gaze to the sand. The clouds above him were moving with a serene rapidity that taunted the moon above them and sent her light in ripples as through a sieve onto the haunting water below. He tugged at his sleeves for warmth and caught the wound on his wrist, sending searing pain shooting through his beleaguered body. Clutching it to him he raised his head in a wince and his eyes found the sea once more.

Jacob, slumped alone and crying - his vacant inbox open on the computer screen beside him; an abattoir, where all his defenceless past pets hung, flayed from a hook in the ceiling; a dark hooded figure with a glinting gun, racing through an unfamiliar forest, taking aim; Alec, snake's tongue protruding from his thin white lips, advancing on a willing Isla; a ripple on the water's surface. Wait. That ripple was really there. His hyperhallunications dissipated in an instant and he widened his gaze, breathing harder than ever.

'Please,' he rasped, 'don't be a mon-' but he stopped short. There, a few feet away from where he saw the ripple, a small black shape rose from the water. Though the night transforms even the mundane into the mysterious, Leo was calm and his mood instantly lifted by this unexpected show. For, illuminated in the moonlight, he recognised the shape which floated on the surf.

'You're out a bit late!' he said, and a grin surprised his frozen face.

He knew seals were plentiful around these islands, but had never expected to come across one at night-time: especially not one exerting the same characteristic curiosity. How much could those big black eyes see? Still, strange as it was, he had a companion.

'Are you alone too?' Leo whispered to the seal as it bobbed beneath and above the waves at regular intervals, turning its head this way and that.

'Of course you're not.'

A single tear, the first he'd shed since he ran away, wound its way down his ghost-white face - a raindrop on a glacier - and left a trail of warmth in its wake. He sniffed and instinctively wiped his eye with his lower palm. When he looked back at the sea it was quite dark. The clouds had clustered together to block out the lunar lamp and he could not discern anything beyond the shoreline.

Leo was steadily beginning to feel more like himself, the cold marine air draining the intoxication from him, and he thought of setting off for the tent. Nothing would feel so bad in the morning. He hoped. But he wished to have one final glimpse of the seal before leaving. Looking to the sky he could see a gap in the clouds, large enough to accommodate the full moon for a few minutes. That would give him long enough to satiate himself for tonight. So he pulled his legs in close to his chest and rested his chin on his knees, eager to say farewell to his visitor.

A chill wind ruffled through Leo's tousled, unkempt hair and he reached up to the back of his head to shield himself from the worst of it. At that moment, the vast expanse of the beach began to light up as if a helicopter searchlight was shining systematically upon the desolate sand as the moon emerged from behind her shroud. He watched expectantly, preparing a miniature monologue and decided to categorise everything he could determine about the appearance of this seal - so that he would recognise it if he saw it again.

Then the light passed over him. For a few moments he thought he saw the seal raising itself further above the waves and was quite taken aback. What if they were dangerous? What if it shot out of the sea and caught him. Bit him. Sank its sharp teeth into him. Into his leg. Into his arm. Into his wrist. Into his wrist.

'OWWW!'
The acute pain he'd imagined the bite would produce suddenly materialised. As had happened on his birthday, his wrist scolded as if the air were lava scorching letters on his flesh. With his left arm he grasped his right below the affected ring and squeezed tightly as the pain intensified. His teeth crunched together as he ground them, a hissing sound emitting - unwillingly - from his mouth. Watching in horror he shrieked as flakes of his skin dissolved away and blood dripped down his arm.

'AHHHHH!!!! NOT AGAIN!!!!! WHAT. THE. HELL. IS....????' he shouted.

Helplessly he rocked himself backwards and forwards as more of his greyblack blood trickled down his arm and onto the sand beneath. Second after second his wound was changing. What had once been a rash, turned to slashmarks in elegant lettering. Now, before his unbelieving eyes, the letters slowly began to glow.

'ARRRRRGGGGGHHHHHHHH!!!!!!!!'
The sensation of a thousand injections simultaneously puncturing his wrist accompanied the glow. He lurched over, lightheaded, his eyes rolling into his head. He was going to pass out. Too much pain. The terrific light seemed to absorb him once more. There was nothing he could do. His face hit the soft, dark sand and he curled into a crumpled ball. Any second now he would succumb, he knew it.

In the distance the lapping of the waves grew stronger. As his sight was lost, his hearing compensated. Mostly, he heard his heart beating inside his head. The wind skirted his figure with its awful howl. Any second now. Any second.

Then his heart froze. Something was moving over the sand. Something. The squelchy thuds, barely audible over the roar of the sea and the hum of the wind moved with a menacing lack of speed.

THUD.

Leo was silent, his breathing erratic.

THUD..................... THUD.

He tried to look, but all was darkness.

THUD......DRAAA.... THUD.
....THUD.

No, he'd run for it. He'd get up. He'd. He lifted his head from the sand and angled his knee beneath him.

'ARGGGHHHHHHH!!!!' his wrist responded with a lightning shock, keeping him in agonising semi-paralysis, writhing desperate and blind on the ground.

The pace of the steps quickened. This was it. Whatever it was was only a stride away. It was closer. Leo could hear deep rattling breaths, furious and sharp.

The steps had stopped. Whatever it was was looming over him.

Leo felt an incredible need to be sick. Never. Why him? What had he...? Why?

His hearing began to fail. The light grew brighter. Somewhere in the distance he felt an icy liquid splash over his arm......

The Court Convenes

Deep underground, somewhere in Central London, 12 suited figures sat stiff in their high wooden chairs. In front of them, was a long mahogany table was covered in papers, scruffily arranged in piles, blue folders and the odd ring-binder resting readily beneath a sturdy hand. Enveloping them, the windowless wooden-panelled walls were as plain as they had been for centuries. The only light in the room came from globes embedded into the three enormous golden ceiling fans which dangled precariously above. Beneath these lamps, the room had the aura of a pool-hall. Manoeuvring himself carefully into the correct position to pot the black and conclude the game, the Prime Minister narrowed his sights in earnest.

'Tell me, Johnathan, how is the weather in Wales at this time of year?'

'I wouldn't know Sir,' boomed Johnathan, a slim, hirsute man, sat furthest away from the PM, 'I'm always here!'

A cacophony of laughter erupted from all those in the room.

'Quite.... quite right..' chuckled the PM, whose seat was, naturally, at the head of the table.

'Though I am assured by the forecasters that it is rather awful.'

'Typical.'

'Yes, Sir.'

'Knowing that, have you given any thought to where you might honeymoon?'

'Sir?' asked Johnathan, colour draining from this face.

'Your honeymoon?' smiled the PM, 'Come on, you didn't think I wouldn't know did you?'

'I..... I.....'

'Oh, enough of that.' said the PM with a flick of the wrist. He then sniffed loudly, and sat up straight.

'Now, as you all know, our commercial interests have seen a downfall of late -'

'Foreigners!' called one of the members.

'Savages!' called another.

'Yes, yes, thank you. If I may continue, this is largely due to the activities of modern states in which we do not hold a large enough position of influence.' Lifting a pen to his lips, he paused for a few seconds, his deep blue eyes scanning the room. When, finally, his eyes came to rest on a short woman with shoulder-length hair that curled inwards like a scythe - he removed the pen from his mouth and tapped it three times on a folder that lay splayed on the table.

'As already mentioned, I have informed the Parliament that it is their duty to increase the revenue stream, at no matter what cost. I believe they are devising an intricate system of tax hikes and cuts in their services for the masses. Ultimately though, it falls to us during this unprecedented time, to preserve our very being. We need to actively consolidate our position. We have allowed ourselves to become far, far too relaxed and we shall soon all be paying the price. Our programmes need to be sped up. Our investments cashed-in and redistributed. Our holds need to be strengthened. You all know what this means.'

The other suited figures all began to nod.

'If we are to remain Great, we are going to have to-'

A knock emitted from the heavy wooden door.

'Enter!!' shouted the Prime Minister, his face contorted and reddening.

The door creaked open to reveal a tall fresh-faced girl with hair the colour of straw.

Pushing her headset microphone out of the way of her mouth she said:

'They've located him, Sir.'

The Prime Minister stood up immediately, signalling the others to do so as well and there followed a great scraping of chairs.

'Anthony,' he said hurriedly to a tall, dark man on his right, 'as Chief Passanter, this is your mission. Go.'

Without a word the man dashed off through the door.

'This sitting is over. See you all in a week.' shouted the PM, letting his face fall into a hesitant smile.

They left in conspicuous silence, halfmarching to the exit until only one remained - stuck at the back of the pack. The PM then bolted forwards, and closed the door before her.

'Y..Yes, Sir?' said the woman, startled, and flicked her auburn hair over her shoulder.

'Sarah,' sighed the PM, 'see to it that Johnathan and his.... *wife* .... do not live out the night.'

'Done, Sir.' she replied, expressionless.

He gave her an appreciative nod, and opened the door handle for her to pass.

Revelations

'Halo!' someone shouted distantly.

'Halo!' it came again, this time filtered by a gentle whirring, a constant noise like the buzz of a computer. Leo groaned. He felt a hand on his shoulder. Shaking. He was dizzy. Damp. Freezing. Where was he? He couldn't remember falling asleep. Slowly, as if they'd been thawing out, he opened his eyes, flicker by flicker. Around him was nothing but blur. A vista of paintwater, spreading and swirling with different tones, corrupting the purity. Another shake roused the body from his sleeping mind, his sight normalised and he shifted his gaze downwards.

Immediately he jumped backwards, scrambling to move away. Before him was a boy, about his age. Yet this stranger was stranger still. The boy, down on one knee, was completely naked from head to toe and glistening wet in the moonlight. His eyebrows were raised slightly and his breath a steam that was absorbed into the surrounding air. Whilst staring at the boy, immobile with shock, his arm throbbed and he realised, gratefully, that it was no longer the intolerable torture of before. Still, his breathing was fast and erratic. This was no monster, but he could be monstrous.

'*Ciamar a tha sibh?*' said the boy, and he moved closer to Leo.

Leo stared blankly back, unable to understand.

'*Is mise* Lysander.' he continued, and looked expectantly at Leo.

Leo opened his mouth to speak, but no words could form. He'd just caught sight of the boy's eyes, penetrating through the darkness. His irises were perfectly white, encircled in a ring of black. But it couldn't be. There was no-one. In all the years the doctors had looked. In all the medical journals.

'*De an t-ainm a th'oirbh?*' the boy said, speaking slowly and at an ever higher volume.

'I....I... ' Leo managed to mutter, '..I don't... under*stand* you...'

The boy's eyebrows knitted together and his eyes narrowed. He stood, slowly and gracefully, exposing more of his pale, dewy skin, his sides marred by scars. The wind picked up around them once more and whilst Leo, battered by the ardent frost, quaked and winced though fully-clothed - the boy stood resolute: as blissfully ignorant as if it were a warm summer's breeze.

'You speak like them?' he said in a strong accent, glaring down at the quivering Leo.

'I? Them....? I don't know what you're talking about,' replied Leo, his racing mind stumbling at every hurdle.

'There's no need to play the fool. I've seen your *tearmann*. I know what you are.'

'My... what?'

'Your *tearmann*. Why did you let it cause you so much pain? You could have died.'

'Look,' said Leo in anguish as he pushed himself up so a seated position, 'I don't know what a *tearmann* is, I don't know who you are and I certainly don't know who or what you think I am. My name's Leo Hall, I'm 18, I'm here because I ran away from home when my parents told me I was adopted. I'm an orphan. I was kidnapped that night, stuffed in a van with a dismembered deer and chased with a gun when I escaped. Then I find a letter telling me where my orphanage was. I go there and they have no record of me. I no longer have an identity. Everything, to date, has been lies. So, please, if you really know who I am then do me a favour and TELL ME!!'

Leo's eyes welled up through the last sentence and he struggled to get it out. He was near breaking point, he knew it. He'd never spoken to anyone like that before. The revelation prompted silence from the boy for a few moments. He shifted his weight between his feet and crossed his arms.

'You really don't know what you are?'

'What do you mean, what I am? I know *what* I am. I'm human, male-'

'No, what you *really* are.'

Leo felt every inch of his body at once. His heart slammed into his throat and the blood in his arms churned, churned, churned. He shook his head.

'You're an *Atharannach*.' Leo stared up at him, blank-faced. 'A shape-shifter.'

'A... a what?'

'A shape-shifter. We *Atharannach* can turn ourselves into animals.'

'So....wait a minute. I can turn myself into any animal I want?' Leo grimaced.

'No. Just one. Which one on the other hand is another matter.'

'Well, what can they be?'

'No one knows how many of them there are. There are writings, legends of an exact number, but there are also rumours of more.'

'How about you? What are you?'

'Me?' the boy smiled, 'I'm the best kind.'

Leo wondered how long this joke was going to go on for. There must be a video camera somewhere. This would be up on the internet within hours. A smash hit viral. Nude Scottish lad humiliates pasty, hungover English boy.

'Oh yeah, what's that then?' Leo asked cockily, looking around for the telltale red light of a video camera on record.

'I'll show you,' said the boy, and he dropped to his knees before spreading himself out on his front.

Of course he would. He'd show Leo how-

Just then something started to happen to the boy's skin. Leo thought his eyes were going blurry again at first. But no, there was no explaining this away. His skin had started to turn brown. His face, still plastered with a maniacal grin, looked as though it were covered in boot polish. Presently everything became more grotesque. The brown skin now rippled like the water's surface racing from a stone. Clicks and crunches sounded out from the boy as his body shortened, his legs fused together and his arms were sucked back into his skin. Ripple after ripple his body expanded, his torso becoming larger and larger.

At the last change, Leo could bear no more, and threw up onto the sand behind him. The grinding of shortening bone was coming to a stop now, and with one last turn of the head, the boy's face disappeared. Morphing into the short snout, black eyes and razor sharp teeth of the animal he'd become.

Leo was alone on a deserted beach on a lonely island, not two feet from a fully grown adult seal. He jumped up to his feet, which finally, given the heavy dosage of adrenalin they'd received in the last few hours, seemed to be responding. It couldn't be true. Couldn't. There was no way this was real. Yet there it was, staring him in the face. He'd always felt different. Always. He'd always known there was something. Something. He thought he'd found out why. He was adopted. That was why. He was from a different stock. His genes weren't right. He couldn't. Couldn't. Couldn't.

Eyes wide with terror he started to walk away from the seal, towards the tent. He'd get back there. They were normal. He was normal. He was still normal. They'd be fine. He'd be fine. He grabbed his hair and pulled, desperate to extract his thoughts from his head.

Running up behind him came the creature, back in human form. He reached out and grabbed Leo's shoulder, who shook his hand off.

'Hey!' shouted the boy.

'I don't..... want.... anything...... to do.... with...' said Leo angrily, not turning round, nor stopping.

'Too late! You're one of us whether you like it or not.' He was jogging to keep up with Leo now, 'Where are you going?' he exclaimed, 'Back to those humans? You think they'll accept you? Sooner or later you'll learn their true colours. Sooner or later you'll be abandoned, too much of an outsider. Too different. Worse still, they find out what you are - you're done for.'

The words rang through Leo's head like a bullet cutting through the air. They had already abandoned him.

'What do you mean?' asked Leo, turning to face the boy, who was quite dry now, though covered in sand.

'There are so many things you don't know Leo Hall. You're lucky to have survived this long.'

'What don't I know?'

'You don't know anything, and that is exactly why you will end up dead in a matter of days if you go back there. Unless you can learn to control your shifting, it'll happen outside of your control, when you least expect it. That pain you felt in your arm today? That's nothing compared to being shot by a hunter's bullet. Trust me.'

'So....' Leo shook his head. This was all a bad dream, '...so *what* then?'

The boy did not reply straight away, but instead looked stared out at the horizon. Dawn was coming.

'I can help you. I can show you all you need to know.'

'No, I don't want your help, I just want to go *home!*' shouted Leo, and he turned, racing off ahead.

'I can help you find your real parents!'

The words smacked Leo over the head like a spade and he stopped, silent. Slowly he turned to face the boy and frowned at him.

'Why... why would you do that?'

'Because..... Because I know what it's like to feel alone...... Because, I don't want to see yet another meaningless *Atharannach* death.'

Right hand grasped tightly over the steering wheel, Anthony reached across to the passenger seat. Retrieving his packet of cigarettes, he removed one and put it in his mouth. Changing gear with a hard crunch that made the entire vehicle lurch, he threw the packet back to the empty seat. As he awkwardly lit his cigarette, his black eyes looked to the road ahead. There was one other car, in front of his, and beyond - the slumbering giants of Skye, foreboding in the impossible silver light. The bridge that stretched out before him, raced by as he hit the accelerator. There was no time to lose.

'You're alone?' croaked Leo, 'But what about those other seals I saw yesterday?'

'They were exactly that. Seals.'

'What about your family? Where are they?'

'My father was killed by a ghost net. A fishing net that humans recklessly abandon. Once trapped, there was no way out and he drowned.'

'Oh, I'm sorry...' said Leo, his voice descending into a whisper.

'My mother, well, she was taken.'

'Taken?'

'By them. *Leomhann:* a group of humans that hunt our kind, determined to wipe us all out.'

Through a dense fog of anxiety, things were beginning to fall into place in Leo's mind.

'We.... we're *hunted?'*

'Have been for centuries. The only way for us to live is to remain in our animal form for most of the time. Or at least, that used to work. Now they're coming for us, singling us out from the other animals. Targeting us first. No- one knows how.'

'..But why.... why would they hunt you.. I mean us... I mean... we're like them!'

'Humans don't think like that. We're different. We're a threat. I couldn't tell you exactly what started it. There is some literature that speaks of it.'

'You have literature?'

'We may look like mere animals. But once, we were so much more. Our writing is everywhere. If you know where to look. There are verses on mountains, beneath pools, on trees - all nearly invisible to humans.'

'Invisible? How?'

'Look at your wrist.' He pointed at Leo, and then held up his own. 'And mine.'

Through the healing wound, Leo could see a luminescent bracelet of intricate letters cascading around his wrist. He looked up at the boy's and saw his, brighter, pure, no scabs or scarring.

'That tattoo is in lunar ink. It glows only in moonlight. That ink is what our literature is written in. Or at least, all our *shared* literature.'

'This is a tattoo?!' Leo was incredulous.

'Yes, it's your *tearmann.* Each shifter child has their individual *tearmann* tattooed on them in lunar ink after birth. It documents your name, your tribe and a traditional verse. It is supposed to protect us.'

Leo thought that his hadn't done him a lot of good so far. In fact, he wished he didn't have one. Was inflicting pain on children their cultural pastime?

'So why has it never shone like this before?'

'I don't know. Mine shone the first time I saw moonlight. I was surprised when I saw the wound on your arm. When I saw you in pain. That is what happens before your first shift, normally. I had mine when I was a baby.'

The reflection of the black 4x4 rushed along the shopfronts. Swiftly the vehicle passed through the dead of night, its tinted windows and lack of numberplate aiding its camouflage. Anthony looked to the electronic screen mounted above the stereo. Concentric rings emanated from a blue dot that was static on the coloured map. He was closing in.

'What's your name?' Leo asked the boy. The sky was beginning to lighten now to the east, dawn would soon be here.

'I've tol-' said the boy, before remembering that Leo could not understand his language. 'I'm Lysander.'

'Cool.'

'Haha,' Lysander smiled, though his eyes were far away, 'Can I ask you a question, Leo?'

'Er, yeah, go ahead.'

'How did you survive being taken?'

'What? I wasn't taken.'

'You said you were kidnapped.'

'I was human.' He thought of the back of that awful van. Dismembered carcasses, strewn across the floor. The instruments. The blood. The smell. 'S...surely they can't?'

Lysander nodded, his face frozen and blank. 'They can.'

Leo suddenly became very aware that they were both out in the open. If what Lysander said was true, they were leaving themselves as easy targets. Hadn't he been out in the open when he was kidnapped the first time?

'I... I found a gun in the back of the van I was in, and I, I shot the door open. I ran.. I.' he started fidgeting, '... listen, I don't think we should be here.'

'If anyone was coming for us Leo they would have come by now.'

'Yeah....' said Leo, unconvinced, and he looked in every direction. 'Yeah.'

'I didn't think it was possible. I thought that once you were taken that was it.'

'Well.... it wasn't it for me.' said Leo, desperate now to be anywhere but on this beach.

'So it might not be for her.' said Lysander, glassy-eyed.

The tracks from the road led away to an old overgrown path. If he went down there, his target would flee. His black leather boot crunched down hard as he began the ascent of the mound of rock and sand before him.

'Listen, how did you do that before?' asked Leo.
'Do what?'
'Change... shift into your animal form?'
'It's easy!'
'Please tell me,' Leo begged. If he was able to change now, whatever he could turn into might give him half a chance at getting away from here unnoticed. They knew what he looked like.

'Well, you just picture your animal inside your head and keep your focus on it. Then you change.'
'Great. I won't be able to do it then.'
'Why not?'
'Because I don't know what animal I am, do I?'
'Did you listen to anything I said before?'
Leo thought that he'd mainly paid attention to the parts where Lysander had told him he was being hunted.
'What?'
'Your *tearmann* tells you your tribe.'
'And?'
'And your tribe is your animal.'
'But I can't read it!'
'I can, give me your arm.'

Lysander reached out for Leo's arm, and roughly pulled it towards his eye level.

'Hah! I knew it.'

'What?'

'You're a deer!'

Leo felt as if he were inside a Dali painting. This was the most surreal experience he'd ever had. He was not only a boy of 18. He was also a deer. A *deer*.

'A deer?'

'Well, a stag.'

Feeling slightly better, Leo retrieved his wrist from Lysander's hold.

'So I just need to think?'

'No, first you need to strip.'

'I'm sorry, what?!' Leo exclaimed, his eyebrows raised.

'You need to be naked. Those clothes aren't going to fit you when you're a deer are they?'

'But I'll freeze! And...... you're here.'

'Trust me, you don't have anything I don't have. Not yet anyway. And you won't be cold once you're covered in fur.'

'And what about when I change back?'

'Are you going to move your clothes?'

'No.'

'And neither am I. So if you want to change, strip.'

Feeling profoundly self-conscious, Leo did so. His clothes tearing at his cuts and scrapes which had still not fully healed.

'There...... d...d... done' said Leo, shivering.

'No you're not.'

'Wh....what are you talking about..?'

'Since when did you see a deer wearing socks?! Get them off.'

Taking his hands outs from under his armpits, he did so, reluctantly. The damp sand soon sending shockwaves of cold throughout his body.

'Good. Now you're going to want to get down on all fours.'

'Do what?'

'You can stand up if you like, but you'll only hurt yourself - more.'

'What do you mean more?'

'You'll find out.'

The icy wind was making Leo convulse.
'C'mon, the longer you stand there human, the colder you'll get!'
Finally, feeling like main attraction in some ludicrous circus, Leo dropped to the sand.
'Now, picture a Red Deer stag in your mind. Doesn't have to be doing anything. Just think of it. And focus,' said Lysander, as he began to walk in a circle around Leo.
Leo could focus on nothing but the cold which was devouring his milky skin and turning his fingers blue. He tried to picture a Red Deer and instead a fire blossomed in its place. A roaring fire that emanated beautiful, healing warmth.
'Close your eyes and *focus*!' ordered Lysander.
He closed his eyes and imagined a deer in his mind. The deer from the other night. Noble, tall, striding. Nothing was happening. He imagined it running, bounding over hills, and clashing with another male in rutting season, its breath painting the air.
'It..... isn't....' he muttered 'wor-'
An intense heat spreading across his body stopped his train of thought. His neck began to rotate of its own accord. He breathed faster as his insides began to churn, his navel twisting like he'd been possessed by an untalented belly-dancer. He felt his ears close up and could no longer hear the sea.

CRACK

A savage pain shot through all his limbs and he tried to scream, but nothing came out. He felt himself raising slowly off the floor, agony coursing through his arms as they stretched. He watched helplessly as his hands shrank and the skin grew tough and hard and he cried out silence as they ripped apart to form two brown hoof-like toes. The cold was no longer present and through the torture he felt quite warm. A splitting pain not unlike a condensed migraine shot through his head and he winced, eyes closing, and stumbled forwards. A steadily increasing weight above his ears forced his head into the sand. Slowly his hearing returned and the pain began to subside. He stood unsure on spindly legs and used all his strength to rear his head. When he did so, he opened his eyes.

Lysander was standing near him, still as a waxwork and nearly as lifelike. The light had spread across most of the sky now, and the first arc of the sun was visible across the horizon. Lysander's face was stern, his lips slightly parted.

'No....' he whispered, 'Something's wrong.'

Anthony lifted the heavy black gun into position as he advanced down the beach-side of the hill. Placing the sight to his eye he drank in the image of the two figures below. There, unmoving in the timid morning light, a naked youth stood beside a large, unwieldy Stag. He placed the crosshair over the beast, and giving his quarry no warning - pulled the trigger on the great White Stag.

*